T0369434

Dawnelle Salant

Order this book online at www.trafford.com
or email orders@trafford.com

Most Trafford titles are also available at major online book retailers.

Note for Librarians: A cataloguing record for this book is available from Library
and Archives Canada at www.collectionscanada.ca/amicus/index-e.html

Printed in Victoria, BC, Canada.

ISBN: 978-1-4251-3268-2 (sc)
ISBN: 978-1-4251-6993-0 (e)

*Our mission is to efficiently provide the world's finest, most comprehensive book publishing
service, enabling every author to experience success. To find out how to publish your book,
your way, and have it available worldwide, visit us online at www.trafford.com*

Trafford rev. 10/19/2009

www.trafford.com

North America & international
toll-free: 1 888 232 4444 (USA & Canada)
phone: 250 383 6864 ♦ fax: 812 355 4082

For my Grandpa, who smiles at me every day from heaven.

CHAPTER ONE

W hen Stacy Myers arrived home from school one Tuesday afternoon, she had no idea that she was about to make a remarkable discovery that would change her seemingly dull life. Before this day, she would never have guessed that cleaning her room could be so rewarding.

"Stacy! Clean your room right now!" Stacy's mom's voice reverberated throughout the entire house. "I don't want to see your face until that room is spotless!" Stacy's mom had been after her for weeks, months even, to keep her room tidy. It was not that Stacy was a naughty child; she usually followed all the rules, ate her vegetables and did her homework on time. She just could not keep her room tidy.

She honestly did try. Sometimes she would think about tidying up, then find something that had been lost for days, which usually meant that she would become distracted. Thus, the job was never finished.

Today, though, was a little different. Stacy was preoccupied with her best friend Jade's birthday party on Saturday. She was only allowed to go if her room remained up to her mother's standards until then. Saturday was four whole days away and she knew it was going to be a challenge.

Gritting crooked teeth, Stacy trudged down the hallway

to her room, tripping over the stubborn corner of carpet that would never stay down. At least she had the best room in the house - that was one of the advantages of being the eldest child. Her little brother, Danny, had a tiny room right next to the bathroom, but Stacy's room was spacious with a lovely window overlooking the gigantic, green backyard. She often spent hours staring out through this window, daydreaming about far away and mystic places.

When Stacy arrived at her room, she glanced through the window and noticed a beautiful bird sitting on the branch of the nearest tree. Without even thinking about it, she sat down on her purple beanbag chair and watched the miniature blue bird singing away. That was when she noticed the novel she was reading and picked it up, intending only to read one or two pages.

An hour later, Stacy's mom found her in the exact same spot, still absorbed in her book. "Stacy! What do you think you're doing? You've been up here for an hour. You should have at least started on your room by now. There'll be no TV for you after dinner today, and none until this room is immaculate!" Thanks to Stacy, her mom was now running late for her yoga class. She warned Stacy that her room had better be spotless before she returned, or there would be no birthday party.

Every Tuesday, Mrs. Myers put on her tights and carried her thin, blue mat out the door. She returned about an hour later, always looking much more relaxed. Tonight, because Stacy's dad was out of town on a business trip, their teenage neighbour, Brenda, came over to watch Stacy and her brother. Before she ran out the door, Mrs. Myers said to Brenda, "Make sure Stacy stays in her room until it's clean!" Stacy shrunk back and hugged the wall with embarrassment.

Stacy's mom looked a little less peaceful than usual as she made her way up the driveway after class later that night. She probably suspected that she would find Stacy's room just as messy as she had left it - and she was right. A new computer game had caught Stacy's attention, and she would have still been engrossed in it, had she not heard the car door slam. Stacy considered hiding, but she knew that would only make things worse. She wondered how an hour could slip away so easily; at school, an hour seemed like forever, but at home playing computer games, it seemed like an instant.

Like most normal ten year olds, Stacy owned oodles of things. Toys, CD's, clothes, books and knick-knacks from various trips covered her bedroom floor. Stacy's white dresser was covered with barrettes and scrunchies that she used to tie back her long, brown hair. Sometimes she remembered to put her books on their shelf above her desk, her clothes in the basket and her teddy bears on her bed, but mostly, they lived on her floor.

Stacy didn't really see a problem with this. Her room was messy, not dirty! She always cleaned up after herself in the kitchen. She would never leave dirty dishes in her room and nothing that would smell or grow was ever left under the bed.

Stacy's bed was always made, but this was only because it was Stacy's favourite part of the room. She took great pride in pulling her deep purple comforter up over the purple and white striped sheets, and neatly placing the multi-coloured cushions at the top of the bed. If only she could keep the rest of her room as neat as she kept the bed.

Stacy really began to panic as her mom got closer to the door. She jumped around and waited for a brilliant idea to save her social life. In the end, she ran to her door and slammed it shut. Short of a genius plan, Stacy began shoving everything under the neatly made bed. Several minutes later, there was a loud knock on the door.

"Stacy? Honey, it's me, I'm home. Are you finished? Can I come in?" It was her mother.

"Just a minute! I'm nearly done. There, that's it," panted Stacy. "Come in!" She managed to shove the last bit of a sweater under the bed, and grabbed the last book off the floor. There was nowhere left to put it, so Stacy sat on the bed and pretended to read.

"Well," exclaimed Mrs. Myers, pleasantly surprised. "I see you have been working hard! I was wrong. I expected to come home to a…Hm. What's this?" At the last moment, Stacy realized that the arm of her favourite teddy bear was sticking out from under the bed. Her mom gave it a tug and it slid out easily. The only problem was that a t-shirt was tangled up in its ribbon, and the t-shirt was stuffed into a backpack, and the backpack unfortunately had two shoes tied to it, and the shoes had some old socks inside. Mrs. Myers was a smart woman. She knew that the rest of Stacy's mess was still there; it just couldn't be seen.

"Young lady! My dear, silly, little girl. I won't say much. You know that you've made a big mistake. This was your last chance. You know what will happen now that you've chosen not to complete this one task I left for you." Stacy's mom was calm, but sometimes this was worse. Stacy knew she was in for it.

"But I really did mean to do it! Mom, it's not fair! It's my room; I should…" stuttered Stacy, but with one look at her mother, she knew not to push it. She had made her choice, with a little help from the computer, and now she would have to suffer the consequences.

"You won't be going to Jade's birthday party on Saturday, and until this room is cleaned properly, you won't be allowed to watch TV or play any computer games. Is that clear?" Mrs. Myers asked, her hands placed firmly on her hips.

"Yes," answered Stacy, and turned her back so her mom wouldn't see her tears. Ten year olds don't cry when they get in trouble. "I'll have it cleaned by tomorrow," promised Stacy. Her mother just nodded and quietly closed the door behind her.

Tears continued to run down Stacy's cheeks. Not only had she made her mom angry, which she hated to do, but now she would miss the party of the year. Jade's parties were always the best. This year Jade had convinced her mom to allow them to go swimming and have a sleepover. How would Jade feel? "I've really made a mess of things," Stacy muttered to herself.

SMILE

Only two weeks ago, Jade and Stacy had had a fight. It was a minor fight, but to a ten year old, any disagreement can mean the end of the world. It had all started with Kimberly - the most popular girl in Stacy's class. Kimberly is flawless; she can correctly answer any question the teacher asks, she makes everyone laugh, she lives in a big house, she wears expensive clothes and travels all over the world with her rich parents during the holidays. If that's not enough, her big, blue eyes and shiny, blonde hair make her one of the prettiest girls in the whole school.

Because Kimberly is so intelligent, she can get people to do whatever she wants. She is slightly bossy, but everyone does whatever she asks because they all want to be her friend. Stacy and Jade have a secret agreement not to fall under Kimberly's spell, but when Kimberly wants something, it can be hard to say no.

The previous week, Kimberly had hosted a party at her gigantic house with her ballet friends, and Jade was the only one from school that she had invited. "Please don't go! You won't be my true friend if you go to her party!" Stacy had begged Jade.

But Jade, like everyone else, secretly thought that Kimberly was the coolest person in the school. Who wouldn't want to go to her fancy house, eat her sumptuous food and look at her designer clothes? So naturally Jade went. But she didn't tell Stacy, and when Kimberly blabbed about it the next day at school, Stacy was distraught. Luckily, the problem was resolved when Jade admitted that she didn't have a very good time anyway, and that Kimberly's ballet friends were dreary. Stacy and Jade had promised to remain best friends forever.

After the party, Jade had half-heartedly tried to convince Stacy that Kimberly was actually quite nice, but relented when Stacy brought up the Mandy incident. Neither of the girls would ever forget the time that Mandy, another girl in their class, had come to school with a very bad haircut. Mandy used to have nice, long chestnut hair, but had to cut it short when she joined the swimming team. When Mandy had arrived at school without her glossy hair trailing down her back, Kimberly couldn't keep her mouth shut.

"Mandy? Is that you?" she had squealed with laughter. "Or maybe we should call you Andy now! You look more like a boy than a girl!" Although most of the other kids found Kimberly's comments amusing, Mandy didn't, and she ran away with tears streaming down her cheeks. Stacy would always remember the look of sadness on Mandy's face as she tried to cover her head with her hands. Stacy wondered if she had that same look on her own face right now.

Later that night, Stacy finally pried herself from her bed, wiped her tears and managed to put a few things away. She picked up her favourite blue sweater and held it to her chest. It still smelled like vanilla from the cookies she had shared with Jade the last time she wore it. The colour matched Stacy's eyes perfectly and Jade always told her that she looked very pretty in it. What would Jade say when she found out that Stacy couldn't come to her party? Stacy made a vow to keep her things where they belonged so she would never have to go through this again. All her friends managed to keep their things neat. What was her problem? She just wasn't good at it.

Just like Math. Stacy was smart enough, but put a set of numbers in front of her and her mind went blank. She just couldn't add, subtract, multiply or divide to save her life. Every day at 11:00, during math class, Stacy wanted to turn invisible. She usually spent the whole hour praying that she wouldn't be asked a question. Stacy would never forget the day that Miss Terrence, her teacher this year in Grade Five, asked her what ten times ten was. She knew that the answer was 100 – that was an easy one - but Stacy was so nervous that she answered 10. All the children laughed at her, and Stacy had never felt so embarrassed in all her life.

In any case, she would worry about Math tomorrow. Stacy had a job to do now. She began to pull things back out from under her bed. She put them away one by one and she soon found that her room looked much better. To help make the time go by faster, Stacy put on her favourite CD, by SMILE.

SMILE was the hottest group around. All of the singers were Stacy's age and they always dressed trendy and sang fun, catchy songs. What Stacy really loved about them was the way the band got their name. The members of the group were Sarah, Matthew, Isabella, Lara and Eddie, and the first letters of each of their names spelled SMILE.

Listening to music really helped Stacy make progress on her task. When she was almost finished, she got down on her hands and knees to take a good look under the bed. There were only a few things left on the far side, right up near the wall. But try as she might, Stacy could not reach those last few bits and pieces. She stretched and twisted and turned, but she just couldn't get at them. The only solution was to move the bed.

After a lot of pushing and shoving, the bed was finally far enough away from the wall for her to grab the book, socks and towel that were jammed there. But when she grabbed for the towel, Stacy realized that it was caught on something and wouldn't come out. She briefly considered leaving it there - it was only one towel, how could her mom be mad about that? Then she thought about Jade's party and how much she wanted to go. Maybe her mom would change her mind if she worked extra hard on her room.

Resigned, Stacy got up and gave the bed another big shove. It moved all the way into the middle of the room and Stacy was free to work on the towel. Just then, there was a knock on the door. "I *am* cleaning my room! Leave me alone!" yelled Stacy, thinking it was her mom checking up on her. Instead, her brother flung open the door and sat down on her bed.

"Whatcha doin?" he said.

"What does it look like? I'm cleaning my room," Stacy said. "Get out! I don't need you in here making more of a mess."

"Do you want to play a computer game with me?"

"Danny, I can't." Stacy softened. "I got in trouble for my messy room again and I can't use the computer or TV until it's clean."

"Oh," Danny said, looking sad.

"Look, I'm sorry. If you let me finish, then maybe I can read you a book or something after. Okay?" Stacy didn't like to see her brother sad. He was only six, but he was a good kid and they had a lot of fun together.

"Good luck, Stacy," Danny said seriously on his way out.

Stacy went back to work on the towel. As she tugged at it, Stacy realized that the towel wasn't caught *on* anything, it was caught *in* something. A trap door, to be exact. "I didn't know that there was a trap door in my room!" breathed Stacy. "Wow! I wonder where it leads?" She lifted the heavy, wooden door very gently, pulled out the towel and let the door drop back down into place. Her heart was hammering an uneven rhythm against her chest. What if something scary was under there? A ghost? A robber? Who knows what could be lying in wait. Stacy quickly pushed the bed back, put her last few things away and got ready for bed. Danny's book would have to wait until tomorrow.

As Stacy reached to turn the light off, her mind returned to the trap door. *There could be something scary under there*, she thought, *or something really cool. Like treasure! A chest of gold or a magic book that would teach me everything I need to know about Math! Maybe I should open it.* Stacy paused as an idea came to her. *I know, I'll tell Jade about it tomorrow. She'll know what to do. We can open it together.* With this happy thought, Stacy rolled over and tried to sleep. Her mind kept returning to the trap door; she wanted desperately to see what was under it, but she knew it would be even more exciting to wait and share it with Jade.

CHAPTER TWO

The next morning, when Stacy's mom barged into her bedroom to make sure she was awake, Stacy groaned and protested as usual. She pulled her head back under the thick covers and tried to hide - until she remembered the trap door and her plan to discuss it with Jade. With one quick motion, she jumped out of bed and bounded into the bathroom, surprising her mother.

"Something exciting must be happening at school today," Mrs. Myers said.

"No. Just a normal day," Stacy lied. "I'm only trying to do what you tell me and get up on time. I don't do everything wrong, you know".

"I know that Stacy, and your room does look very good. Why didn't you just do that in the first place? Then you'd be going to the party on Saturday with all of your friends."

Stacy got dressed and went downstairs where she ate her breakfast silently, hoping her mom would utter the magic words, *Okay, you can go to the party on Saturday*. But Stacy didn't hear them.

When she got to school, Stacy ran straight to the swings on the playground where she met Jade every morning, but Jade wasn't there yet. *That's strange*, thought Stacy, *Jade is always here before me*. While she waited, she planned exactly what she would say to Jade and how they could convince their moms to let Jade come over after school. The trap door just couldn't wait!

A car pulled into the parking lot, and Stacy ran over just as Jade was opening the door. "Jade!" Stacy shouted. "Come here! Quick!" Stacy started running over to her friend, but stopped when she saw Kimberly getting out of the car too. "What? No!" Stacy cried. This couldn't be happening! Jade would never do that to her. Stacy dropped her books and ran into the bathroom, tears pouring out of her big, blue eyes.

When the bell rang ten minutes later, Stacy had stopped crying, but she was still shuddering from what she had seen. She walked into class without looking at anyone and sat down in her seat. Her books were on her desk but she didn't know who'd picked them up for her. She didn't hear a word that Miss Terrence said, and all she could think about was Jade and Kimberly together. It didn't make sense. Why did they come to school together? Stacy decided that she didn't want to know. If Jade wanted Kimberly as a best friend, that was fine, she could have her.

While her teacher droned on and on about plants and chlorophyll, Stacy couldn't help but remember the time that she and Jade had decided to plant an apple tree in Jade's backyard. Jade's dad had been planning to help them, but he had been called into the office at the last minute. Stacy and Jade decided that they could do it by themselves, so they each got a shovel and started digging a hole together. It wasn't long before they were both covered in dirt and blisters. They dug for over an hour, but the hole was barely big enough to hold a single rose, never mind an entire tree.

Stacy was just about ready to give up when Jade hit something hard with her shovel. Both girls got down on their hands and knees to see what Jade had found. After they had cleared the dirt away, they could see a big boulder wedged in the dirt, right where they wanted to plant their tree. Jade's older sister, Fiona, came out to see what they were up to and offered to help them move the boulder. The three of them were able to remove it, but not without a lot of huffing and puffing. With the boulder gone, the small tree fit in the hole perfectly and Fiona held it steady while Stacy and Jade put the dirt back to hold it in place.

That was a year ago. During the summer the tree had blossomed with beautiful white flowers, and eventually grew seven apples. They weren't very big, but they tasted even sweeter because Jade and Stacy had planted the tree together. Once a week the girls got together and watered the tree and made sure no weeds were growing near it. *I guess Kimberly can help Jade take care of the tree now*, Stacy thought.

At lunch, Stacy sat with Trinh, Lacey and Christina. They didn't ask why she wasn't eating lunch with Jade, they knew. Trinh and Lacey looked over to where Jade and Kimberly sat eating together, and saw that Jade looked a little uncomfortable. "Why do you think Kimberly has picked Jade as her new best friend?" asked Christina. "She always tries to steal someone's best friend, but it never works. Jade will be your friend again soon Stacy, I just know it!"

"Yeah, well, I don't really want her back. They might as well stay friends. I'm fine without her. You don't mind if I eat with you from now on, do you?" asked Stacy.

"Of course not," the three girls chorused.

Briefly, Stacy considered telling them about the trap door. That would really teach Jade! "If I tell you something, do you promise to keep it a secret?" whispered Stacy.

"Yes!" the three girls leaned in so they could hear this big secret.

They looked very excited and Stacy said, "Last night………. last night, I," and stopped. She just couldn't do it. It wouldn't be the same as telling Jade. She could see Jade's face when she heard the news, see her eyebrows go up in that funny crooked way that they did when she was excited, and she quickly changed her mind about telling the secret. "Last night I had a big fight with my mom. I can't keep my room clean and she's really mad at me. Do you guys keep your rooms clean?"

Looking a little disappointed with the secret, the girls launched into their own stories of fights with their moms, but Stacy wasn't really listening. She couldn't keep her eyes from wandering over to Jade's table. It was hard not to notice that Jade did look a little sad. When she looked Stacy's way, Stacy turned her head back towards Trinh and laughed exceptionally hard at her silly story.

————————————

At dinner that night, Stacy's mom was very talkative. She felt bad because Stacy seemed so sad, although she was sure it was because she had to miss Jade's party. If only she knew that Stacy had completely forgotten about the party and was thinking only of Jade's new friendship with Kimberly.

"How was school today?" Stacy's mom asked her.

"Fine," replied Stacy.

"Did you learn anything new?"

"Not really."

"What did Jade say when you told her that you couldn't go to her party?"

"Oh," Stacy paused, "Nothing. I didn't tell her. Jade's not really my friend anymore."

"What? Of course she is!"

"No, Kimberly is Jade's best friend now."

"What happened?" But Stacy didn't feel like talking about it and she didn't answer her mom. She just wanted to finish her dinner, go upstairs and open the trap door. Alone. She didn't care what she found now, nothing could be worse than her day at school.

"May I be excused please?" Stacy asked. When her mom nodded, she ran upstairs to the privacy of her own room. As Stacy reached her room, all of the sadness and anger that she had been holding inside all day finally burst out and she collapsed on the bed, crying. After about ten minutes, she felt a little better and sat up and looked around. Her eyes landed on the telephone and she jumped up, ready to call Jade and make everything okay. Maybe there was a good explanation for why she had come to school with Kimberly this morning.

She picked up the phone, dialled, and then hung up. What would she say? What if Jade didn't even want to talk to her? Or worse, what if Kimberly was there? They might be doing all the things that Stacy and Jade did together; like play games, practice SMILE's dance moves, or eavesdrop on Fiona's conversations with her boyfriend.

Jade was so amusing, and so much fun to be with. Stacy and Jade had been friends since they were three years old, and Stacy never had as much fun when she was with any of her other friends. No matter where they went, or what they did, they were always smiling when they were together. Especially during sleepovers - the two girls would stay up all night talking and giggling. Jade had slept at Stacy's just last weekend and even after all the lights had been turned off, they whispered until they were too exhausted to keep their eyes open.

"What do you want to be when you grow up?" Stacy had asked Jade.

"A princess."

"Me too!"

"Then we can live in the same castle together and wear long, pink dresses and grow lots of apple trees!" Jade loved to make up stories about princesses, dragons and swords.

"Do you really think there are still princesses?" Stacy brought Jade back to reality.

"Hm. I don't know. Maybe."

"You could write books about princesses and go around to schools reading your stories to little kids," Stacy suggested. Jade loved to help people; she was the most considerate person that Stacy knew.

"Maybe if I can't be a princess, I can be a doctor. I like to take care of people," whispered Jade.

"You took good care of me when Rotters got lost." Last year, Stacy's cat, Rotters, had gone out and never returned. Jade had drawn a beautiful picture of Stacy and her cat, and brought her a blossom from the apple tree. Jade's thoughtful actions had made Stacy feel better instantly.

"Okay, you can be a doctor. But what about me?" Stacy moaned. "I can't be a princess without you!"

"Yes you can!"

"How?"

"When I'm not busy with my patients, I'll write a book about Princess Stacy, and then we can turn it into a movie and you can be the star!" The two girls giggled.

"Perfect!" Stacy had declared, but now she wondered if Princess Stacy hadn't been replaced by Princess Kimberly.

Stacy decided that she couldn't call Jade; so instead, she sat back down on the bed and thought about what she should do. She could wait and see if things were better tomorrow - maybe Jade would explain everything and they would be best friends again. But things might get worse. "Could I get through another day not knowing what is under there?" Stacy asked herself. "No! I can't!" With that, she jumped off the bed, pushed it away from the wall and clasped her fingers onto the trap door handle. She stopped, thinking of what might be below, and backed away. Then she got her courage back, ran over, and gave it one big tug. Up it came...

CHAPTER THREE

All Stacy could see at first was one or two stairs, and then darkness. A funny smell emanated from down below, a smell that Stacy recognized, but couldn't quite place. It made her tongue feel dry. She hesitated for only a moment and then took a deep breath. Delicately, she placed her left foot on the top stair. She waited. Nothing. She lifted her right foot and placed it on the second stair. Again - nothing. She could see that the stairs kept going for quite some distance.

Her heart hopping with exhilaration, Stacy put her foot on the third stair. She was surprised that she wasn't scared anymore - only excited and curious. Slowly, carefully, she made her way down the stairs. The smell was getting stronger and Stacy tried hard to identify it. For some reason, it reminded her of the summer that she had spent at the beach house with her family.

Stacy must have taken ten steps when she decided to look back up at her room, but to her surprise and dismay, she couldn't see it anymore. There was a slightly lighter spot somewhere in that direction, but she couldn't be sure that it was her room. She thought about turning back - it still wasn't too late. But what did she have to go back to? Her mom was mad at her, her best friend was no longer her best friend, and her impossible math homework was waiting for her on the desk.

Stacy continued down the stairs. She took two more steps when her foot suddenly hit water. She pulled it back quickly and shook off the moisture. As soon as her foot got wet, Stacy realized that the smell was fish. Not the kind of fish you'd order in a restaurant, but the fresh smell of fish that you can only get at the seaside. Curious, she put her foot back in the water. *Just one more step* thought Stacy as she put her other foot down.

Her foot dangling over the last stair, Stacy made a decision. As much as she liked to swim, she didn't think she would like swimming in the stairway under her bed, when no one knew where she was. But by the time she made her decision, it was too late. Stacy could feel the force of the water sucking her down. She tried to scream but all that came out was, "Grgl," as her head was submerged. Stacy's heart beat out of control as the cool wetness covered her from head to foot. She didn't even have time to think about breathing, she was pulled in that fast. She was holding her breath and squeezing her eyes shut when the most fantastic feeling came over her.

It started at the tip of her head and slowly worked its way down to the tips of her toenails. It was sort of a warm feeling - tingly and gentle all at once. Whatever nervousness Stacy had felt vanished in an instant. She relaxed enough to open her eyes, and when she did, she accidentally opened her mouth because what she saw was astounding. She could taste salt, and her mouth hung open for several seconds before she realized that she wasn't holding her breath.

In fact, Stacy wasn't even thinking about breathing anymore. Although she knew that she didn't have to worry about air, she didn't fully understand that she could breathe underwater. All she knew was that the pain in her chest was gone and she wasn't gasping for oxygen. Stacy could only concentrate on what she saw in front of her.

The view reminded her of an aquarium she had once owned. It was as if she was looking at the ocean through a freshly washed window, but she was truly right there in the middle of it all. To her left, Stacy saw movement and quickly turned her head just in time to see an enormous fish swim by. The long, silvery grey fish zipped through the water as if something was chasing it. *A barracuda*, Stacy thought. She may not be good at Math, but she loved the ocean and could name almost any underwater creature.

The weird sensation Stacy had felt earlier was beginning to fade. She felt completely normal and perfectly at home in her new underwater environment, so she decided to have a look around. She had been floating in one place since she'd opened her eyes and she wasn't sure how to move around. Should she walk? Should she swim? Stacy pushed off from the sandy bottom and swam toward the spot where she had last seen the barracuda. She was amazed at how easy it was to move around in the warm water. Her body felt light and swimming required very little effort. For the first time in two days, she felt completely relaxed and her mind drifted away from all of her problems.

Stacy couldn't believe the colour of the water. It looked as if it had been painted with Stacy's favourite Crayola crayon; Cerulean Blue. As she swam along, Stacy saw beautiful shells on the sandy bottom. She had collected a lot of shells during her summer at the beach and wanted to add more to her collection. She swam down and picked up a huge conch shell. Although it was very beautiful, it was also extremely heavy. She quickly put it back and looked for something a little smaller. Near the huge conch was a lovely oyster shell that would fit in her pocket. She reached down to pick it up, but stopped suddenly when she heard someone speaking to her.

"Hey, you shouldn't take things that don't belong to you, you know."

"Who said that?" asked Stacy.

"Me! Up here!" Stacy looked up and saw a small, grey dolphin swimming toward her. "How would you like it if I went into your house and took some of your things?" asked the dolphin.

"Well, I am in my house," said Stacy. "I think."

"Not anymore you're not. The ocean belongs to my friends and me. You can't take that, I'm afraid. It's a part of the ocean and moving it could destroy our balance. That was someone's home once, you know. It's there for a reason. "

"Oh! I'm so sorry," said Stacy. "I will leave it where it is. I promise I won't touch anything else. I just thought that it was beautiful and that it would look really nice on my shelf."

"Very well. I know you didn't mean any harm. In any case, it's nice to have a visitor. No one comes around much anymore. What's your name? I'm Amanda. Welcome to the ocean."

"Are you a bottlenose dolphin, Amanda?" asked Stacy.

"Why, yes I am!" exclaimed Amanda. Stacy could tell that Amanda was happy that Stacy knew what kind of dolphin she was.

"My name's Stacy and I love the ocean. If I promise not to touch anything else, would you show me around? I would love to meet some of your friends!"

"I think that could be arranged. Follow me!"

Stacy followed Amanda with great anticipation. She loved the water, she loved swimming and she loved sea creatures. This was like a dream come true! Good thing she'd found that trap door, otherwise she would have missed all of this. She didn't stop and think how strange it was that the dolphin was talking to her. She was too happy to let anything ruin her blissful adventure.

They swam for about ten minutes and passed many gorgeous fish. Stacy saw yellow and black striped angelfish, blue and green parrotfish and even one scary, brown lionfish. They were the most spectacular colours that Stacy had ever seen. She was surprised to find that even her favourite colour - purple, was down here at the bottom of the ocean. One angelfish had purple and blue stripes. Another one was only black and white, but its designs made it just as pretty as the colourful fish. She wanted to stop and play with them, but Amanda kept rushing her.

Just when Stacy thought she could swim no more, Amanda

started to slow down. She could see a figure up ahead and wondered what kind of creature it could be. She hoped it wasn't anything scary, like a shark! As she got closer, Stacy saw that the shape kept moving. It was round at the top, but she couldn't make out the rest of it. *It must have five or more legs,* thought Stacy. Then, out loud, she said, "Of course! It has eight legs! It's an octopus!"

"Stacy, I would like you to meet my friend, Oliver," said Amanda.

"It's lovely to meet you, Oliver," said Stacy. "But I thought octopi only came out at night. It's only the afternoon. Shouldn't you still be sleeping?"

"Well, I was sleeping until Amanda woke me up," Oliver yawned. "But that's okay, I love meeting new friends, especially ones who know so much about the ocean!"

"I think you and Amanda are very lucky to live here. You have a beautiful and exciting home,'" said Stacy.

"You haven't seen anything yet! Come this way," said Oliver speeding off. Amanda followed quickly and Stacy had no choice but to swim along after them.

I wonder who I'll meet next? Stacy thought happily as she swam along behind her new friends. She didn't have long to wait, because Amanda and Oliver stopped and motioned for her to come closer. They had stopped near a stony cave and Stacy swam up slowly. There could be anything hiding in the cave, and for the first time, she felt a little scared.

"Come on, Stacy! Don't be scared!" shouted Oliver. "It's another good friend of ours."

"Jeffrey won't hurt you - I promise. He's very old and he doesn't move very fast anymore. Come see!" encouraged Amanda. Stacy swam up. She could see something green just sticking out of the mouth of the cave.

"Green? What sea creature is green?" asked Stacy. "Oh! It's a moray eel, isn't it?" she exclaimed with delight. She had never seen one before, not even at the aquarium - only in picture books. Jeffrey looked like a long, thick, green snake. He had a

SALANT

big mouth and two small, beady eyes. Stacy moved in closer for a better look, but this seemed to scare Jeffrey. He ducked back into his cave and wouldn't come out.

"Jeffrey? My name is Stacy. I'd really like to see you. I think you're the most beautiful shade of green that I have ever seen! Would you please come out?" Stacy waited patiently, but nothing happened. "Wait a minute! Don't moray eels like to eat octopi, Oliver? Is it safe for you here?" asked Stacy, worried.

"It's okay, Stacy. Jeffrey and I are good friends. We go back a long way. He's too old to chase after me now anyhow!"

"Okay. If you're sure." She turned back towards the cave. "Jeffrey? Please come out again!" begged Stacy.

"Jeffrey is a little shy," said Amanda. "He might stay in there for the rest of the day, but at least you got a glimpse of him."

"Yes, well I would like to see him again but I'm sure there are other things you can show me!" Amanda and Oliver smiled at each other and quickly swam off.

Stacy was getting tired. Swimming around in the ocean that she had discovered under her bed with talking sea creatures was turning out to be very hard work! As she plodded along, Stacy could see something swimming towards them. It looked fairly big and Stacy felt her heart do a somersault, but she knew that her new friends wouldn't take her near anything dangerous.

"Hello!" called the big shape, which was getting closer and closer.

"Hello!" called Amanda and Oliver. By this time Stacy could see that the shape looked an awful lot like a shark. Not a big scary shark, but a shark nonetheless.

"Stacy, this is our friend Julia. She's a nurse shark," said Amanda.

"Don't worry. She's harmless!" said Oliver after seeing the look on Stacy's face. But when she heard the words, "nurse shark" Stacy had already relaxed considerably. She knew that nurse sharks weren't dangerous to humans at all. In fact, Stacy had seen TV programs where people went swimming with them.

"Hello, Julia. I'm Stacy. It's nice to meet you!"

"Hello, Stacy. Welcome to our ocean." Julia offered Stacy a fin. Stacy wasn't sure what to do, so she took the fin in her hand and gave it a little shake. Just think, a few hours ago Stacy was in her room crying over her lost friend, and now here she was shaking the fin of a nurse shark!

"Ooh! Your skin is very rough," said Stacy. "Can I touch your back?"

"Of course," replied Julia. "Just be gentle!" Stacy ran her hands over Julia's rough back. It felt just like the sandpaper her dad used to smooth wood in his workshop. Thinking about her dad made Stacy think about the fight she'd had with her mom. Her mom! What if she was looking for her and found the trap door?

"Amanda, Oliver, I think I should be going home now. I don't want my parents to worry about me! How do I get back?"

"Oh, you don't really have to go do you? We're just getting to know each other!" said Amanda.

"I know, I don't want to leave either, but I have homework to do. I promise I'll come back tomorrow, and every day after that!"

Stacy turned to Julia and said, "It was nice meeting you. I hope to see you again!" Then to Amanda and Oliver she said, "Let's go!" Amanda and Oliver led the way.

As Stacy swam on with her new friends, she looked over to the right. They must be going back the same way they came because she recognized Jeffrey's cave. *Wait*, thought Stacy, *Jeffrey is looking out!* She waved to him and watched carefully to see what he would do. Slowly he started to grin at her. He gave her a huge smile, and then, before retreating into his cave for good, he winked at Stacy. She was so happy that Jeffrey had remembered her.

Oliver and Amanda stopped near the place where Stacy had been picking up the shells. "Thank you so much for a wonderful time! I loved meeting all of your friends. I'll come and see you tomorrow, okay?"

Amanda said, "We had a great time too. Thanks for visiting!"
Oliver and Amanda waved good–bye and started to swim off.

"Wait! How do I get home from here?" shouted Stacy.

"Close your eyes and swim to the top. It's easy!" said Oliver.
"Good–bye!"

"Don't leave! I don't know how to get home!" cried Stacy,
but they were already gone. So Stacy did what they had told
her. She closed her eyes, and pushed her feet hard off the sandy
bottom. Five seconds later, Stacy landed on something hard.
"The stairs! I'm back!" she cried joyfully and ran up the stairs
back to her room. She quickly closed the trap door and moved
her bed back. That was when she realized that she was completely dry. *Did that really happen, or did I make it all up?* A knock
at the door made Stacy forget about what she was thinking.

"Stacy?" called her mom. "What are you doing?" The door
opened and as her mom walked in, Stacy's heart pounded. Was
everything back in place, or would her mom find some clue as
to her adventure? "Are you finished your homework Stacy?"
She paused and bent over. "What's this?" She reached down
and picked up a shell - the exact same shell that Amanda had
told her leave on the ocean floor. How did that get there?

"Oh, that's from the summer we spent at the beach. It must
have fallen from my shelf," answered Stacy.

"Well, now that your room is finally tidy, let's try to keep it
that way, okay honey?"

"Yes, Mom," Stacy said, picking up her math book. Some
things never change.

That night Stacy had a dream about Jade. They were frolick-
ing in the ocean with Amanda and Julia. Even Jeffrey had come
out of his cave to play tag with them. Stacy woke up just as she
was about to get tagged by Jade. She smiled to herself as she

imagined chasing Amanda and trying to catch the speedy dolphin, but the smile faded quickly when she remembered Jade and Kimberly's new friendship. She wanted so badly to share the trap door and her new ocean buddies with her best friend. But she knew that wasn't going to happen.

CHAPTER FOUR

The next day was Wednesday, Stacy's least favourite day. She had double Math in the morning and it always ruined the rest of her day. But this Wednesday, Stacy was determined that nothing would ruin her good mood. She headed straight for Jade on the playground to tell her the exciting news. She just knew that once she told Jade about her secret, everything would be all right again.

Jade was standing all by herself on the playground. *Perfect*, thought Stacy. She went running over and when Jade saw her she gave her a huge smile. "Jade! Guess what?" breathed Stacy.

"What?" asked Jade. She looked very happy that Stacy was talking to her again.

"You'll never believe what I found! Under my bed.......there was a trap door.......and the ocean and..." but Stacy had to stop there. She was out of breath from both anticipation and running.

"What are you talking about, Stacy?" Jade suddenly looked angry.

"I found a trap door under my bed," Stacy panted. "There were some stairs so I went down them and I was in this ocean! I met a dolphin. Her name is Amanda and she has a friend named Oliver! He's an octopus and......"

"Would you listen to yourself Stacy? Are you crazy? I don't know what you're trying to do, but if this is your way of trying to get back at me for hanging with Kimberly..........well, it's just not going to work." Jade marched away, leaving Stacy standing there. Kimberly had just arrived so Jade ran over to her and they walked into the school together.

This made Stacy feel worse than she had yesterday. She had been sure that sharing her secret would bring her and Jade closer together, but it had only pushed them farther apart. "Why doesn't she believe me?" Stacy said to herself. She got a funny look from two boys standing next to her, so she decided to go in and review her math homework so her day didn't get any worse.

The big talk in the classroom that day was SMILE. Stacy could hear everyone talking about the band and she knew something must be up. She saw Trinh and Lacey and went over to them. "What's up? Did something happen to SMILE?"

"Didn't you hear?" squealed Trinh. "Sarah quit the band! She said it's too much hard work and she doesn't have time to be a kid!"

"You're joking!" exclaimed Stacy. "If I was in SMILE I would never quit, no matter how much work it was! They're the best!"

"The songs won't be the same without her," moaned Lacey. "She was definitely the best singer!" The bell rang and the girls took their seats for the first math class.

It was horrible, as usual. Stacy kept thinking about Sarah leaving SMILE and Jade's new friendship with Kimberly. She got all of her answers wrong because she wasn't listening. She just couldn't stop thinking about SMILE and her new ocean friends.

Christina joined Trinh, Lacey and Stacy for lunch again and they continued gossiping about SMILE. No one was happy about Sarah leaving the group and everyone was worried that it might mean the end of SMILE forever. That would really suck!

SMILE

Stacy walked home alone that night, very quickly, because she could hardly wait to go swimming in her ocean.

"Hi, Mom! I'm home. I'll go do my homework and then come down for dinner, okay?" said Stacy.

"How was school?" asked Stacy's mom. Stacy told her about SMILE and her mom listened as she started getting dinner ready. Then Stacy was off to her room. "Don't forget to tidy your room after you are done your homework, dear."

"Mom! My room is perfectly tidy. I haven't messed it up at all, and I won't either. I'm learning how to be clean!"

"Oh, that's right," her mom said, with a wink.

Stacy rushed up the stairs, threw her bag on the floor and went straight for the trap door. Forget the homework – that could wait until after dinner! This time when Stacy went down the stairs she had no fear; she almost ran - she was so eager to see Amanda, Oliver, Julia and maybe even Jeffrey! She kept going and going and finally stopped. "I should have hit the water by now!" she said aloud to herself. She took a few more steps, but her feet remained dry. "That's weird. I wonder if I'm going the right way?"

At that moment, Stacy saw a flash of light just a few stairs down and heard music playing. Curious, she took a few more tentative steps and recognized the song as her favourite SMILE hit. A big grin lit up Stacy's face as she hurried towards the music. She could hear cheering and clapping now and Stacy had no doubt that she had walked right into a SMILE concert. This was just as good as the ocean – if not better!

"Stacy? Stacy, is that you?" she could hear someone saying. "You don't want to be late for your first show! Hurry up!"

"It's me, Stacy! Who's there? Who are you?" she said as she hit the last stair. Someone grabbed Stacy's arm and pulled her towards flashing blue lights. As she was being dragged along, Stacy got a good enough look at the someone to know that it was Isabella, who just happened to be her favourite member of SMILE.

"Isabella?" said Stacy incredulously.

"Yes? What is it? Are you nervous?"

"Nervous? What would I be nervous about?"

"Well, it is your first show with SMILE. I was really scared before my first show. Don't worry though, you'll be fine!"

Stacy was confused and couldn't quite think of anything to say to her favourite pop star, so she just followed her down the dark hallway. They soon came to a door, which Isabella opened, leading Stacy into SMILE's dressing room. Eddie and Matthew were sitting at a table playing a game of cards while Lara was fluffing her hair in a mirror bordered by lights. They were all dressed in jeans, white runners and wild purple and blue tie-dyed t-shirts. When Isabella opened the door, they all looked up and cried, "Stacy!"

"It's okay guys," said Isabella, "I found her outside in the hallway. She was just nervous and wandered away."

"We only have ten minutes before we go on stage, Stacy, "said Lara, "we'd better get you dressed!"

"Wh- wh - what do you mean, go on stage?" stammered Stacy. "I'm going on stage with you? With SMILE?" Stacy didn't know whether to laugh or cry.

"Of course, silly! You're part of SMILE now!" said Lara, leading her into a separate room full of pretty clothes.

"Sarah quit the band and you came to the audition, remember?" asked Isabella.

"No, not really, I mean, um, I'm not really a very good singer……..am I?" asked Stacy as she pulled on a pair of jeans.

"You're a wonderful singer, Stacy, or else you wouldn't be in the band! So was Tess, the other girl who auditioned, but we couldn't exactly ask her to be in the band could we? We'd have to change our name to TMILE!" joked Lara.

"I promise! You'll knock 'em dead out there tonight!" said Isabella. "Just remember, Lara and I are taking all of Sarah's lead parts for tonight and you just have to sing background on the chorus. Just like we practiced, okay?"

"That way you don't have to worry too much about singing and dancing together in your first show," added Lara. At the mention of dancing, Stacy's heart dropped. She may be unsure about her singing ability, but she knew for a fact that she couldn't dance. She put on the clothes that Lara had handed to her, and glanced at herself in the mirror.

"Okay. I think you're ready, Stacy!" declared Isabella taking Stacy's hand in her own and saying, "Good luck!"

"Let's go!" cried Lara and the three girls went to join Eddie and Matthew who had just finished their card game.

"Group hug!" cried Eddie and all four members of Stacy's favourite pop band nearly crushed her as they surrounded her in a massive bear hug. Stacy was still reeling from this when everyone joined hands and headed for a door with a sign that read, "TO THE STAGE." Stacy's heart felt like it was going to jump right out of her chest and bounce all over the floor.

When the door opened, Stacy was blinded by the lights and paralyzed with fear. Matthew and Eddie ran straight out on the stage and jumped around waving to the crowd, but Isabella and Lara stayed behind with Stacy for a few extra seconds. "On the count of the three we'll go together, okay?" said Lara.

"Just enjoy it, Stacy! It's a lot of fun!" added Isabella.

"One, two, three!" said Lara and the three girls joined hands and ran out into the pink spotlight shining on the middle of the stage. Stacy was so blinded by the pink light glaring in her eyes that she couldn't even see the crowd. She looked over at Isabella and Lara and saw that they were waving and smiling at the audience, so she did the same.

Five microphones were lined up at the front of the stage and SMILE took their positions, ready for their first song. Stacy's eyes were still adjusting to the bright lights and she was suddenly aware of how hot they were making her.

"Hello everybody!" Lara said into her microphone.

"Welcome to our show!" said Matthew. "It's a very special night!"

"Why is that, Matthew?" asked Eddie.

"Because it's Stacy's first show," said Isabella, pretending to swat Eddie over the head with her microphone.

"Let me introduce to you the newest member of SMILE – Stacy!" said Lara pointing to Stacy and clapping. The entire audience stood up and started to clap and cheer while Stacy stood there open-mouthed. *They must like me*, she thought.

"Say something," whispered Isabella.

"Um," said Stacy into her microphone and then moved away when she realized how loud she sounded. "Hi!" she said, this time prepared for the sound of her voice filling the huge auditorium. *There must be thousands of people out there*, she thought, *and they're all applauding for me*. "Thank you! I'm so glad to be here as part of SMILE! I hope you enjoy the show!" Stacy said with a huge grin as the music for the first song filled the concert hall.

Stacy knew all the words and dance routines for every one of SMILE's songs as she had practiced them with Jade in front of her mirror. But this time, instead of a hairbrush, the microphone was real. Being up on stage with the real band was a little different and Stacy wasn't sure that she was going to be able to pull it off. Matthew was just finishing his solo and Stacy knew that the chorus was coming up and she would have to sing pretty soon whether she liked it or not. Stacy took a deep breath, looked over at Lara, who winked at her, then opened her mouth to sing the words she knew so well.

"Dancing and jumping and playing our songs, singing and bouncing all night long, it's time to SMILE! Let us see you SMILE with us!" everyone sang together. When the chorus was finished, Stacy took a step back from the microphone and sneaked a peek at Matthew, who gave her a thumbs up. *I did it*, she thought. *I really did it! I didn't sound so bad after all*..........

After the next chorus came a big dance routine and Stacy was surprised to find her legs moving in time to the music without even having to think about it. *Cross left over right and take two steps back, twirl, jump and back to the start, Cross right over left and take two steps back, twirl, jump and back to the start*.........

Stacy was pleased that the dancing was so easy and natural. "You were right!" she whispered to Lara as the crowd went wild at the end of their first song, "This is awesome! I'm having so much fun!"

"I knew you would," Lara whispered back as she took her place for their next number.

It was a slow song, and Stacy was glad for the chance to catch her breath. Sarah would have usually sung lead on this song, but Isabella and Lara took turns singing the verses and all five band-members sang the chorus together, as in the first song. Stacy didn't have any trouble knowing when to come in and she seemed to hit every note perfectly. *This must be magic,* she thought, *I could never sing like this at home*! Stacy was having so much fun that she almost forgot where she was, but after two more fast songs with even more complicated dance routines, Stacy started to get tired and thirsty.

She saw Eddie go over to a table on the side of the stage and grab a water bottle. She followed him and eagerly opened a bottle and drank the entire contents in one gulp. She would have had another one, but the music for the next song was already starting and Stacy scrambled to take her place at her microphone.

After one more song, the curtain came down and the band rushed back to the dressing room. "Is that it? Only five songs? That wasn't so bad!" said Stacy.

"Oh, it's not over yet," said Matthew, "we just get a break halfway through to rest and change."

"Oh," said Stacy, and she wasn't sure whether to be happy that it wasn't over yet and she would get to go back on stage, or disappointed that she had to go back and continue singing in front of all those people. She was exhausted and couldn't stop squinting from having all those bright lights glowing on her.

"Come on, we've got to get changed!" Lara pulled Stacy and Isabella into their dressing room and the three girls changed into their new outfits.

"You were on fire, Stacy! You didn't make a single mistake!" Isabella said to Stacy. "How do you feel?"

"Well, I'm not nervous anymore, but I'm tired. It's okay

though, I had so much fun!" Stacy said as she pulled on a black knee length skirt. She put on a bright red t-shirt that matched her red runners, and watched as Lara tied up the orange runners that matched her t-shirt. "Why are we all wearing different colours now? I liked the way the other clothes matched!"

"We have so many different clothes to sing in; sometimes they match, and sometimes they don't," said Isabella, who was wearing yellow runners and a matching shirt with her black skirt.

There was a knock on the door. "Ready guys? Time to go back on!" It was Eddie.

"Coming!" called Lara.

"I thought you said we got a rest! I don't know if I can even stand up!" moaned Stacy.

"That was our rest," said Isabella, pulling Stacy to her feet. "Don't worry, once you're back on stage you'll find the energy!"

"Besides, we can't keep our fans waiting, now can we!" joked Lara.

Fans? I have fans? thought Stacy, with a smile. "All right! Let's go!"

As she ran to join the rest of the band on stage, she noticed that Matthew and Eddie were both wearing black pants, but Eddie was wearing a blue shirt and runners, and Matthew's were green. They did match after all - they looked like a rainbow!

After the clapping had stopped and the yelling fans had quieted, the lights shining on the band went almost completely out in preparation for the next song, and Stacy got her first good look at the audience. Most of the people at the show were kids, just like her, having a good time with their friends. Many of them were wearing SMILE t-shirts and hats, and waving banners that said things like, "We love you SMILE!" *This is the kind of thing Jade and I would love to do together*, thought Stacy with a twinge of sadness.

Luckily the first song of the second half of the show was

another slow song, and Stacy had time to get her energy and her smile back before the next upbeat song. Once the music was playing, and her feet were moving, Stacy forgot how tired she was, and her problems with Jade were pushed to the back of her mind. "Can you feel it? Can you move it? Wanna dance with me?" Stacy was belting out the songs like she had been performing them all of her life. *I'm a pop star*! thought Stacy, and she felt as if nothing could stop her.

At the end of the show, the curtain went down and Stacy ran straight for a bottle of water. "Wait! We're not done yet!" called Eddie.

"What?" asked Stacy, as the curtain came back up. The band was back at their microphones and Stacy ran to join them.

"Good night, everybody!" Isabella was saying.

"Thanks for coming!" said Matthew.

"We had such a good time singing and dancing with you!" added Lara.

"What a great night!" was all Stacy could think of saying.

"And don't forget to SMILE!" said Eddie and the band took a final bow and ran off the stage and back into the dressing room.

Stacy sank down onto the sofa and took a big drink of her water. She barely noticed the bottles of Coke and lemonade sitting next to the sweets waiting for them on the table. Lara passed her a brownie and sat down next to her. "What did you think?"

"Of the show?" asked Stacy.

"Yeah, did you like being part of SMILE?"

"Oh yeah, it was awesome. It was really, really fun, wasn't it? I just can't believe how tired I am." Stacy paused and a thought came to her. "Is that why Sarah quit? Because she was so tired?"

"Well," started Isabella. "It's hard to say. It's not easy being in SMILE. We don't get to go to school and do all the normal things that other kids do."

"You don't go to school?" asked Stacy, hardly believing what she'd heard.

"No, we have tutors who study with us on the bus when we're on the road," said Matthew.

"But don't you miss seeing all your friends every day? And what about your families?" Stacy couldn't imagine not going to school every day and seeing Jade, Trinh, Christina and Lacey. Of course, it would mean no more math class.........

"Like I said, it's not easy," added Isabella. "But we do get to do a lot of other fun things, like singing and dancing and sometimes we get to go on TV."

"And we're all friends here. We have fun together and we never get lonely!" said Matthew.

"Don't worry, you'll get used to it!" said Lara. But Stacy wasn't sure that she wanted to.

"Um, I'm just going to go into the hallway for a minute, okay? I need to get out of here for a bit. Be right back!" said Stacy, slipping into the hallway where she had first met Isabella. Without even thinking where she was going, she kept walking and eventually found herself at the bottom of the stairs that she knew led back up to her room.

She stood there for a few minutes, thinking about what to do. She could stay down here and be a pop star, or she could go upstairs and see her family and friends, and maybe even make things right with Jade. Stacy was so tired that she didn't have to think too hard about what she wanted to do. Before she started up the stairs she had a good look around to see if she could find any signs of the ocean and her water friends, but there was nothing to indicate that Amanda, Jeffrey or Oliver had ever existed.

Stacy had just pushed the bed back over her magical trap door when Danny barged in without knocking. "What are you doing? You can't just come in here!" Stacy yelled at him.

"I can do whatever I want! Your stupid SMILE music has been blaring from your room for an hour!" he yelled back. "Dinner is ready. You have to come down. And when are you going to read me a book? You promised."

SMILE

"I'll be right there. Get out!" Stacy was so tired from singing and dancing that she didn't think she could even go down the stairs to the kitchen, never mind do her math homework or read Danny a book. She wondered if her mom and dad had heard her SMILE concert.

CHAPTER FIVE

When Stacy's alarm went off the next morning, she reached over and turned it off without even thinking about it. Her mom nudged her half an hour later. "Stacy! You slept in! Get up. We're leaving in ten minutes."

"What?" moaned Stacy and rolled over to look at the clock. "Yikes! Sorry, Mom, I'll get dressed and be right down." When Stacy got out of bed, she noticed that her entire body was aching. *It must be from dancing*, thought Stacy as she watched herself try one of the dance routines in her mirror. *I really can't dance*, she thought, *what happened on the stage last night*?

"Don't forget to brush your teeth!" called Stacy's mom from the bottom of the stairs. "And hurry up!" Stacy quickly brushed her teeth, washed her face and threw on some clean clothes. Her mom was waiting in the car with a granola bar.

"Sorry, but if you get up late, this is all you get for breakfast!" her mom said.

"That's okay. It's my fault," Stacy admitted.

"Look at your hair, honey!" Even from the back seat Stacy could see strands of her long hair sticking up everywhere. "I'll fix it at school," Stacy sighed. Her mom started the car. One of SMILE's songs was playing on the radio. "Oh," squealed Stacy, "my favourite!" and she started singing along. "Dancing and jumping and playing our songs, Singing and bouncing all night long, it's time to SMILE! Let us see you SMILE with us!"

"Knock it off, Stacy!" cried Danny. "Your singing sucks!"

"Danny, be nice to your sister!" chided their mom.

But Stacy thought, *no – he's right. My singing does suck! But I sounded so great last night!*

At school Stacy had to walk right past Jade and Kimberly who were standing at the edge of the parking lot. "Wow Stacy! What's wrong with your hair? Having a bad hair day?" called Kimberly. Stacy turned just in time to see Jade give Kimberly an elbow. As Stacy walked off, she could hear Jade calling after her.

"Stacy? Stacy?"

She whirled around and met Jade with mean eyes. "What do you want?"

"Well, it's just that your hair is a bit messy this morning. Do you want me to help you fix it?" Jade paused, then asked, "Is everything okay?"

"Yes, it's fine, great actually, thanks for asking. I woke up late and forgot to brush my hair. That's all. Look, Kimberly's calling you. Wouldn't want to keep her waiting now, would you?" Stacy said and marched off.

Stacy went to the bathroom where she did what she could to make her hair look presentable, and then went to class looking for Trinh, Christina and Lacey. She entered just in time to hear Lacey saying, "I think her name is Stacy!"

"What? Are you talking about me?" asked Stacy.

"No, the new girl in SMILE. Her name is Stacy, just like you!" said Trinh.

"What? How do you know?" For a minute, Stacy let herself believe that maybe last night had happened; maybe she was a real pop star!

"It was on MTV last night - they had their first concert to-gether. It was great! Didn't you see it?" Christina practically squealed. "Stacy is so pretty! She has long, blonde, curly hair and she sings just as well as Sarah did!"

"No, I uh, I was busy," said Stacy and she felt her heart sink into her stomach. It wasn't true after all.

"I can't believe that Sarah ever left the group. How stupid! She had it all!" said Lacey.

"Yeah, well it's hard work you know, all that singing and dancing! And they don't get to see their families all the time. It's not easy being a pop star!" Stacy retorted.

"Yeah, cause you would know what it's like to be a pop star, wouldn't you Stacy?" said Kimberly, who had just walked into the classroom. Stacy glared at her and took her seat just as the bell rang. She hardly heard anything that her history teacher was saying about their new unit on Ancient Greece.

At lunch, Stacy apologized to Trinh, Lacey and Christina. "I'm sorry if I was rude this morning. I, uh, I didn't get much sleep last night and I'm just really tired."

"That's okay, Stacy, we know you didn't mean to be rude," said Lacey.

"And don't worry about what Kimberly said, she doesn't know what she's talking about," added Trinh.

"I know," said Stacy, "but thanks." But she did worry about it. She worried about it all day and she worried about what Jade must think of her too. *She's not going to want to be my friend if I keep coming to school with crazy stories and bad hair,* thought Stacy on her way home.

When she arrived at her house, all she wanted to do was fall asleep on her bed, but she knew that she had a lot of homework to do. Since Stacy couldn't (and now didn't want) to go to Jade's birthday party on Saturday, a family outing to visit Stacy's Grandma had been planned for the weekend. That meant she had to finish all her homework tonight, even though it was Friday. If she got it all done before dinner, afterwards she would be free to go down the stairs once more to see what was waiting for her. It had to be good, and let's face it - it couldn't get any worse than real life.

Stacy worked hard on her homework, but she just couldn't get Jade out of her head. That morning, Stacy had seen Jade nudge Kimberly when she was saying mean things about Stacy's hair. That must mean that Jade still cared about her. *Maybe I'll call her*, thought Stacy. *It'll be easier to talk to her on the phone than at school.* Stacy started dialling Jade's number, but gave up halfway through and went back to her homework. After another ten minutes, she put down her pencil, picked up the phone, dialled, and took a deep breath when she heard the first ring.

"Hello?" It was Jade's mom.

"Hi! It's Stacy. Can I talk to Jade?" Stacy was excited now. She knew she could make everything okay if she could just talk to her best friend.

"Oh, Stacy, I'm sorry. Jade's not here. She's spending the night at Kimberly's. I'll tell her that you called."

"Oh. Okay. Thanks," said Stacy, brushing away a tear as she hung up the phone. *At least I have another adventure to look forward to*, she thought as she picked up her pencil.

Stacy was just finishing her homework when she heard the front door open. She had been waiting for her dad to get home from his business trip all week and she could finally hear his voice downstairs. "Dad!" cried Stacy as she ran down the stairs into a big hug. "I missed you!"

"I missed you too, monkey!" he said, with a big smile. "But what's this about you not going to Jade's birthday party tomorrow? Something about a messy room?"

"Oh, yeah, well it doesn't really matter. I don't care anymore. And my room is clean! It has been for three whole days! Go look for yourself!"

"What do you mean you don't care? Three days ago, missing Jade's party was the end of the world!" said her mom. "How quickly things change!"

"I'm sure Kimberly will be there and I don't want to go anyway," Stacy said with a scowl.

"You and Jade still aren't talking?" Stacy's mom looked aghast. "And what's wrong with Kimberly, anyhow? Do you even know her?"

Stacy thought about it. "Well, not really, I guess," Stacy admitted. She put her hands on her hips. "But I don't want to. Okay?"

"No, it's not okay. You're being very childish about this. Why can't you all be friends?"

"Because Kimberly thinks she knows everything, she's mean and she has a big fancy house and......" Stacy couldn't really think of another good reason not to like Kimberly.

"I'm hungry," interrupted Stacy's dad.

"Well then, let's eat. I made your favourite – spaghetti and meatballs," her mom said.

After a delicious dinner, Stacy finished her last three math questions and was finally ready to go back down the stairs. She was getting really quick at pushing her bed out of the way to get at her trap door. Stacy knew that she probably wouldn't be performing in a pop concert or swimming in the ocean again, but she was even more excited to see what would happen this time. She couldn't imagine what would be waiting for her as she ran down the stairs.

After only six or seven stairs, Stacy found herself in the middle of a big cloud of smelly smoke. She coughed and sputtered from the strong smell of gasoline. The sound of a loud horn blasted from behind her and Stacy turned around just in time to see a train chugging away from the cement platform she was standing on.

Where am I? she thought as she looked around. She could see three or four other trains waiting to be filled up with the thousands of people rushing around. A big white sign with black writing caught her eye and she looked up. "London King's Cross," Stacy read aloud. She looked up at the high, arched roof with glass panels and it made her a little dizzy, so she sat down on a bench She was just about ready to get up and explore when a voice startled her.

"You all right, luv?" said an old man with a strange accent.

"Um, yes, I'm fine thank you," Stacy said once she'd recovered from the fright. "Do you think you could tell me where I am?"

"You're at King's Cross Station. In London. Are you lost dear?"

"Oh! No! I'm fine, thanks!" Stacy smiled at the man and ran off, her head spinning. She'd finally realized that she was in London, England – a whole new country on a whole new continent. Stacy had never been outside of Canada before, and it took awhile for her brain to digest this information.

Stacy walked around the big station for about ten minutes before she finally gave up. There were people rushing everywhere and a few times she had almost been knocked over. Stacy suddenly became conscious of a stiff piece of paper that she had been clutching in her left hand and looked down to see what it was. The small, rectangular, orange piece of paper read, "Travelcard." Stacy had no idea what it was for.

She was starting to feel a little scared and worried when she spotted a map on the brick wall. Well, it looked like a map. It had, "London Underground" written above numerous interconnecting coloured lines. She found *London King's Cross* on the map, followed the blue line attached to it and stopped when her finger came to *Oxford Circus*. "A circus! That sounds like fun," Stacy said aloud and then put her head down in embarrassment when she noticed a lady standing next to her. She was dressed in a black skirt and suit jacket, and wearing fancy shoes with very high heels.

"Are you going to Oxford Circus?" the lady asked.

"Yes, I guess so."

"Do you know how to get there?"

"Not really."

"Well, I'm going in the same direction. If you want, I can show you where to get off the tube," she said, with the same funny accent as the old man on the bench.

"The tube?" asked Stacy. "What's that?"

"That's what we call the trains that run underneath London. Haven't you been on one before?"

"No. This is my first time in London."

"Well, come with me. My name is Karen. You look a little too young to be taking the tube by yourself. Does your mom know where you are?"

"Oh yes, she's meeting me at the circus." Karen looked at Stacy a bit strangely, before starting to walk toward some turnstiles.

"Do you have a Travelcard?" she asked Stacy.

"What? Oh yeah – this?" Stacy showed her the piece of hard paper that she'd found in her hand.

"Yes, that's it. Put it in this slot, go through the doors, and then take your card out on the other side. You'll need it to get back out." Stacy did what Karen said and met her on the other side of the turnstiles.

"Ready?" she asked, leading Stacy over to a line of people waiting to get onto an escalator. Stacy had never seen so many people in her life. After they rode down one escalator, they got onto another one going even farther down.

"Are we going underneath the ground?" gasped Stacy.

"Yes, we are. But don't worry, we're almost there." The escalator stopped and they followed the crowds of people down a long hallway covered in white, blue and red tiles. Stacy could see signs with place names directing people where to go. She saw one that said *Oxford Circus* and said, "Is this the way?"

"Yes, and look! Here comes a train now."

Stacy watched a long, worm-like train pull into the narrow hallway next to the packed platform. "You're right! It does look like a tube!" Stacy exclaimed as she was pushed onto the train by the crowds of people trying to board the tube.

"Stay with me! There you go, we're on, just make sure you hold onto something. Now it's just two stops to Oxford Circus, but you'll have to get off by yourself. I'm going farther down the line. Okay?"

"No problem. You've been very helpful!" Stacy watched all of the people on the train. She could hear two girls talking in a language that she knew wasn't English, and she saw one teenager with blue hair and lots of big, silver earrings in one ear.

"Here's your stop! Get off here and follow the people. They'll lead you to the street!"

Stacy got off the tube and once she was on the platform, turned to wave good-bye to her new friend, but Karen was gone. "Thank you," Stacy said, to no one in particular, and followed the huge crowd of people up another two escalators. When she got to the top she went through the turnstiles, then, finally, she was outside. Stacy had been expecting to see a circus, but what she saw instead was a very busy, ancient looking street. There was no sign of a circus anywhere.

"Excuse me," she said to a nice looking old lady waiting in front of a shoe store, "Where is the circus?"

"What circus, dear?"

"Umm, Oxford Circus I think it's called."

"This is Oxford Circus, luv."

"But, there are no animals, or clowns, or rides or…this isn't a real circus!" Stacy cried.

"No, it's a shopping street. Everyone comes here to do their shopping. Have fun!" the old lady said and walked off, leaving Stacy confused as to why a shopping street would be called a circus. *London is weird*, thought Stacy. *The trains run underground and streets are called circuses.*

Since Stacy had never been to London before, she thought she might as well have a good look around, and started walking up the street. She walked past endless clothing stores with names like *The Top Shop, H &M, Dorothy Perkins and Debenhams.* Most looked like they were selling grown up ladies' clothes so Stacy didn't bother going in to look. She came to an HMV and decided to see if they had the new SMILE CD. When she walked in, a girl came over and asked, "Do you need any help?"

"I'm looking for the new SMILE CD," she said.

"SMILE? I don't think I've ever heard of them. I'll go have a look in our computer and you can have a look at this wall. It has all the latest releases."

Stacy walked up to the wall that was covered in CD's, hoping to spot the latest from SMILE, but she couldn't see it anywhere. All she could see were bands with names like Sugababes, Westlife, Girls Aloud, and Atomic Kitten. Who were they? Stacy gave up and walked back onto the street.

She was surprised at how many people were out shopping. There wasn't any room to stand on the sidewalks, and the stores were all packed with people carrying full shopping bags. Stacy tried to cross the street but just as she was about to step out, a big hand pulled her back. Stacy fell onto her bottom and watched as a big red Double Decker bus went whizzing by.

"Where did that come from? I looked before I crossed the road!" Stacy exclaimed to the man who had just saved her life as she climbed to her feet.

"Yes, but you looked the wrong way, luv. You're not from here are you?"

"No, I'm not. What do you mean, I looked the wrong way?" she asked the man, thinking to herself, *why does everyone keep calling me luv?*

"This is England. Cars drive on the opposite side of the street here. You be careful, you hear?" he warned as he headed off.

"Thank you," Stacy called after him. By this time Stacy had had enough of Oxford Circus. Another red Double Decker bus pulled up and a conductor jumped off the back. "Getting on?" the conductor said to Stacy, looking at the Travelcard that she was still holding in her hand. She looked down at it and held it up to him.

"Does this work on buses too?" she asked him.

"You bet! On you git!"

Stacy hopped onto the bus and made her way up the set of stairs leading to the top floor. She had never been on a Double Decker bus before. She sat down right next to the window and watched Oxford Circus go by. Stacy couldn't believe how old all of the buildings were; they were made of white stone and looked like they were hundreds of years old. And there were still people everywhere; climbing up and down the stairs that led to the tube, going in and out of stores and buses. Where did they all come from?

"Next stop - Trafalgar Square!" called the conductor.

That sounds interesting, thought Stacy, *maybe I'll get off here.* Now that she knew she could use the buses and the tube with her Travelcard, she wasn't too worried. She got off the bus and found herself in a huge square filled with statues, pigeons and even more people. She walked closer to the water fountain in the middle of the square and took a deep breath. She had never seen anything like this! She stood on a dark stain in the pavement, slowly turning in a circle, taking it all in.

To one side was a beautiful old church, built from the same stone she had seen earlier, but this church looked really old and some of the stone had turned almost black with age. A sign revealed that the church was called St. Martin's in the Fields. But Stacy couldn't see any fields; she was in the middle of one of the biggest cities in the world.

She could see more busy streets full of people, red Double Deckers and lots of funny looking old fashioned black cars with signs that read, "TAXI". On the opposite side of the square stood a huge tower with a statue of a man on top, but it was so elevated that Stacy could barely see it. She saw several enormous statues of lions and wished she could climb up and pretend to ride them, but they were much too large.

Behind her was the National Gallery, a fantastic old building with stone columns. She headed for the museum and almost walked through a group of pigeons that had been pecking away at some discarded food on the ground. They squawked as they flew in circles and Stacy covered her head with her arms, laughing. "Sorry about that!" she said to the birds.

When she reached the huge stone steps of the National Gallery, Stacy wasn't sure what to do. She was almost positive that her Travelcard wouldn't get her into the art museum, but she really wanted to see what was inside. When she got to the doors, she was happy to see a sign that read, "Entrance Free." She breezed through the doors and inhaled a big breath of air. Stairs led either up or down, and Stacy chose to go up. She figured that she had been down enough stairs for one day!

SMILE

She wandered through room after room. Each was filled with the most exquisite paintings she'd ever seen. Stacy didn't know much about antique art, but from the signs beneath the paintings, she learned that most of them were hundreds of years old. Stacy spent a few minutes just staring at one painting that covered an entire wall. *It's enormous*, Stacy thought to herself. *How could anyone paint that? And it looks so real!*

The next room that Stacy entered displayed modern art. "Sunflowers!" Stacy whispered to herself. "By Van Gogh!" The only reason Stacy knew about this particular painting was because her mom had a huge poster of it framed in their living room. It was her mom's favourite painting and Stacy really liked it, too. *It's even more beautiful in real life*, she thought. Stacy could see the brush strokes made with the thick paint. *I wish my mom were here to see this!*

A large, noisy group of children bounced into the room and Stacy pried her eyes away from *Sunflowers* to see what was going on. It must have been a school class on a field trip, because they were all wearing what looked like school uniforms.

The boys were clad in navy pants and white dress shirts with blue and red striped ties around their necks. The girls were dressed in navy pants or skirts with white blouses, and they were all wearing navy pullover sweaters that said *Cambridge Lane Primary School* in yellow lettering. They were making a lot of noise and the teacher didn't seem to be very happy.

After another hour of staring at the never-ending stunning art, Stacy decided to go back outside and see what else London had to offer. When Stacy walked out the door she noticed that it had started to rain. A bus pulled up to the curb, and not knowing where it was going, and not really caring, she got on. Again, she climbed to the top so she could see as much as possible, but the rain was fogging up the windows so it was hard to see out. Stacy was sure that there was plenty more to do here. She hadn't thought about going home once, her homework was done and there was no school tomorrow. She was free to explore London!

SALANT

Since Stacy didn't have a clue where the bus was going, she decided to count to one hundred and then get off the bus. Stacy closed her eyes and started counting. Almost as soon as she said *one hundred* in her head, the bus stopped. Stacy opened her eyes and ran out onto the street to see where the bus had brought her.

The first thing Stacy saw was a stone bridge that seemed to be going over a large river. She was standing on the riverbank, and when the light turned green, she looked carefully both ways before crossing the street. She was shocked to see that there were still huge crowds of people on the sidewalks and that the streets were filled with continuous traffic.

A grey stone wall ran alongside the river and Stacy could just see over it if she stood on her tiptoes. *This must be the River Thames*, thought Stacy, remembering from geography class that it runs through the city of London. Stacy was surprised to see how wide the famous river was and how slowly it was moving. She couldn't help but notice that it was dreadfully dirty. The water was a nasty shade of brown and she could see bits of garbage floating along.

Stacy strolled across the bridge toward the other side of the river, where she could see a cluster of buildings. When she was nearly halfway across, she heard four loud chimes coming from somewhere above her head. She looked up to see a massive clock tower. "Big Ben!" Stacy squealed. This was one of the most famous clocks in the world! It was so tall that Stacy's neck protested as she lifted her head to get a better look.

The bottom of the clock was a tall rectangular prism that reached toward the dark, cloudy sky. On each of the four topsides of the tower was a clock face outlined in gold. The bell that chimed the time sat under a pointy roof. Stacy noticed that almost everyone around her had stopped to look up. Big Ben was mesmerizing.

From her spot on the bridge Stacy could see the Thames a little better; it was still dirty and she didn't waste too much time staring at the ugly water. The buildings that she had seen from the other side of the bridge were right next to Big Ben. As she got closer to the clock, Stacy could barely see the top and decided that it looked better from farther away. Stacy read a placard stating that the spectacular buildings she was looking at were the Houses of Parliament.

Everything here looked ancient! These buildings looked as if they had been around for an extremely long time. She walked along the sidewalk next to the Houses of Parliament and couldn't believe how long they were. They stretched on for blocks and blocks. Stacy's favourite parts of these buildings were the thin, pointy towers that spiked up from their roofs.

By this time Stacy was exhausted and plopped herself on a bench to rest. She wasn't ready to go home yet, but she wasn't too excited about wandering around London by herself any-more. Again, she found herself missing Jade. They would have had so much fun together in London!

She decided to make one more trip on the bus and then think about going home. Stacy walked to the end of the street but didn't see a bus coming. She waited for a few minutes and then walked another block, but before she saw a bus, she came to a tube station. *I could go down and look at the map and then I would know where I was going,* she thought, and started down the stairs.

Inside the station, she couldn't see a map, but found an esca-lator going down. She stepped on and closed her eyes for just a second. When she opened them, she realized the escalator wasn't moving anymore, and that she wasn't in the tube sta-tion. She was on the stairs under her bedroom and she could see light peeking through the trap door above her. Stacy trudged up the stairs, covered the trap door and collapsed onto her bed. She fell asleep immediately.

CHAPTER SIX

Stacy woke up early Saturday morning, and before she even had breakfast, she went to find Danny. He was up early too, playing a video game on the Wii in the living room.

"Hi, Danny. What're you doing?"

"Playing a game."

"Oh yeah. Are you winning?" Danny pressed a button on his console and turned to her.

"Whaddya want?"

"Well, I thought maybe I could read you a book now."

"Nah, it's okay. I'm havin' fun."

"Danny, I know you're mad at me because I didn't read you a book before when I promised. I'm sorry. I had lots of homework to do this week. Grade Five is hard, you know!"

"Is it?" asked Danny, with wide eyes.

"Yeah. It is. But I'm finished now and I want to read you a book."

"Okay. I'll go get one."

Danny returned with his favourite book, one Stacy had read to him a hundred times before. They curled up on the big white sofa and Stacy started to read. Their parents came downstairs when Stacy was about halfway through the book and stood watching their two children enjoying some time together. When

Stacy finished, they hugged their kids. "That's what I like to see!" said Mr. Myers.

Their mom added, "It's nice to see you two getting along, and not fighting for once. Come on, let's all have breakfast together before we go to Grandma's."

After breakfast, Stacy and Danny helped their mom tidy up the kitchen while their dad packed up the car. "Dad! Put some more of Danny's books in. I can read to him on the way." It was a two-hour car ride to Grandma's house and Stacy knew that Danny would enjoy some more stories.

"Everything's ready," called Mr. Myers a few minutes later, and everyone piled into the red minivan.

"Let's play a game!" yelled Danny.

"But I brought books to read to you," Stacy retorted.

"Well, we can play a game first and then you can read a book. What game do you want to play, Danny?" Mrs. Myers asked.

"The one with the letters," Danny squealed from the backseat.

"Okay. I pick the letter T. Whenever you see something that begins with T; yell it out and you'll get a point. The person with the most points by the time we get to Grandma's wins," explained their dad.

"But that game's for babies," complained Stacy.

"Yes, but it's Danny's favourite. We can play a more grown up game after," her mom said.

"Tree!" called Danny.

"Truck!" Mr. Myers responded.

Stacy's mom prodded, "What do you see, Stacy?"

"Nothing!" Stacy crossed her arms, pouting.

"Nothing doesn't start with T, Stacy," said Danny very seriously.

Stacy had to smile. "No, but tractor does! One point for me!" They had so much fun playing the game all the way to Grandma's that Stacy didn't even notice that she hadn't read any of Danny's books to him. On arrival, Stacy was declared the winner with 42 points, but Danny was close behind with 37.

As soon as they pulled up to the house, Grandma opened the door and came out onto the driveway to meet them. "Grandma!" called Stacy and Danny, running up to give her squishy hugs and loving kisses.

"Hi, kids! How are you? Don't you ever stop growing?"

"Grandma, you say that every time you see us!" laughed Stacy.

They raced into the house, and immediately, Stacy could smell something delicious. "Did you bake chocolate chip cookies for us?" Stacy squealed with delight.

"That's what Grandmas are for!"

Stacy squeezed her and said, "You're the best Grandma ever!"

"You're spoiling us!" teased Mr. Myers, strolling into the kitchen, grabbing a still warm cookie and popping it into his mouth.

"I want one," cried Danny.

"Now wait a minute. We're going to have lunch first and the cookies are for dessert!" Grandma admonished, slapping her son's hand playfully.

After soup, sandwiches and finally the freshly baked cookies, the whole family crawled back into the minivan. "A new park just opened downtown. I thought we could spend the day there. I think both you and Danny will like it. There's plenty of new equipment to play on," said Grandma.

"Sounds good to me!" said Stacy. She spent the whole afternoon chasing Danny around the maze in the park, pushing him on the swings and racing him down the slides. When it was time to go, they both protested.

"Ah, but I have something just as good planned for the evening!" Grandma said.

"What? What?" asked Danny.

"You'll just have to wait. We're going home now to get changed. You two are filthy!"

After everyone had changed into clean clothes, Mr. Myers drove them all to Stacy's favourite pizza restaurant. "How is school, Stacy?" her grandma asked while they waited for their order.

"It's fine," Stacy said, clamming up.

"That's all she ever says," Mrs. Myers said with a smile. "You won't get her to talk much about school."

"How about Jade?" her grandma probed. "I thought she might come with you today."

"No, Jade's not my friend anymore."

"They're having a silly fight. They'll be friends again before you know it," Stacy's mom explained to her grandma.

Stacy had forgotten about her problems while she was having so much fun with Danny, but now they all came flooding back to her. When the food arrived, Stacy ate her pizza in silence and didn't smile again until her grandma told her what the plans for the rest of the evening were.

"We're going to see the new Disney movie at the theatre, so save room for popcorn!"

"Really! Oh, Grandma, coming to visit you is almost as good as going to London!" Stacy said, without thinking.

"What?" asked Mr. Myers. "You've never been to London, Stacy! What do you mean?"

"I, well, I just…I read a book set in London and I think it would be a really cool place to visit, that's all! What time does the movie start, Grandma?" Stacy quickly changed the subject.

"Soon. I guess we should get going! Everyone finished?" said her grandma, looking at her watch.

The cartoon was set under water and Stacy couldn't help but think of the friends she had made in the ocean. *I wonder if I will ever see Amanda, Oliver, Jeffrey and Julia again?* she speculated. *I can't wait to see what will be waiting for me when I go down the stairs next time.*

That night as she settled into her bunk bed in the room that she shared with Danny, Stacy finally got to read her brother another book. "Thank you, Stacy," he said to her before he fell asleep. "I had fun today. You're a good sister. I'll be your friend if Jade won't." Stacy was touched by what her brother had said, but she knew nothing would ever be the same without Jade.

That night Stacy dreamed that Jade came to find her at Grandma's. Jade told her that Kimberly had moved away and they could be best friends again. Stacy awoke with a smile on her face, but quickly realized that it was only a dream and that Jade still wasn't her friend. She wondered how the birthday party had gone the day before. *I'm glad I wasn't there*, she thought. *I didn't have to see Kimberly.*

The next morning, Stacy's mom poked her head in the door. "Are you two awake?" she asked. "Grandma has breakfast ready."

"What is it? Chocolate chip cookies again?" cried Stacy, bounding out of bed.

"No, I'm afraid not. Get dressed and come down."

A big stack of waffles was waiting for Danny and Stacy when they entered the kitchen a few minutes later. "Yum! My second favourite!" said Stacy.

"Second! What's your first?" asked her grandma.

"Chocolate chip cookies, of course!" joked Stacy.

"Well you can't have those for breakfast!" scolded her grandma. "But I baked some more and you can take them home with you. Maybe you can give one to Jade!"

"Grandma! I told you..."

"Okay. Okay. You can eat them all!"

"Not if I eat them first," said Stacy's dad, helping himself to another waffle.

After breakfast, Stacy and her brother packed their things and took them to the car. "Thank you for everything, Grandma." Stacy said. "I had a wonderful time."

"So did I Stacy, so did I," she said, giving her granddaughter a great big hug. "I love you."

"Love you too, Gram. Bye!"

On the way home they played the same game with the letter J, and Stacy let Danny win 34 to 27.

CHAPTER SEVEN

Stacy wasn't looking forward to Monday morning. She'd had a great weekend, but she knew everyone would be talking about Jade's party at school. When she got out of the car, Jade was waiting for her, her hands placed angrily on her hips. "Where were you?" she yelled. "I thought you would still come to my birthday party! Some best friend you are!"

"What do you mean? Isn't Kimberly your best friend now?" Stacy hollered back. "I couldn't come anyway. I was grounded for not cleaning my room."

"Stacy, your room is always messy!" Jade paused, then seemed to soften.. "Besides, you didn't tell me that."

"Well, how could I when you're always with her! I didn't think you'd want me to come."

"Of course I did! You're my best friend. Stacy, my mom's car broke down last week and she knows Kim's mom from work so she asked her to give me a ride. That's all. But you wouldn't even let me explain!"

"Kim? You call her Kim now? And you're always with her, not just for rides!"

"Well, of course I am! You wouldn't talk to me! And she's nice. You should give her a chance." The two girls looked at each other and Stacy felt like she was going to cry. The bell rang and Jade ran off. Stacy followed with her head down.

During History, Stacy kept looking over at Jade, but Jade wouldn't look back at her. She kept thinking about what Jade had said. *I didn't give her a chance, did I? Maybe it is all my fault.* As Miss Terrence rambled on and on about Athens and Ancient Greece, Stacy decided that she would try and talk to Jade again. At lunchtime Stacy hurried after Jade, but Kimberly caught up with her first. Stacy watched the two of them walk away. *How can she be my friend if she spends all of her time with Kimberly?* Stacy sighed and went to find Trinh and Lacey. Christina was home sick that day and got to miss the Monday morning spelling test.

After school, Stacy wasn't in her usual hurry to get home. Even the trap door didn't seem so exciting anymore. She just wanted to make things right with Jade, but she didn't know how. When she got home, she took Jade's birthday present off the shelf and played with the ribbon. She had bought the present almost a month ago; it was a SMILE DVD. She knew Jade would love it, but she didn't know if she would ever be able to give it to her.

Stacy didn't have any homework for once, so she busied herself playing games with Danny on the Wii. After dinner, she helped her mom with the dishes and went back up to her room. She didn't know what to do. She sat down on the bed and thought about it. *I could call Jade, or I could go down the stairs again.* She felt bad about what she had said to Jade this morning, but she didn't see what else she could do or say. *I'll have to sleep on it*, she thought, *but not until after I have another adventure*, and got up to push the bed away.

The trap door opened easily, as it had done the past three times, and Stacy felt a rush of excitement as she took the first step. She felt warm air as she hit the fourth step and wondered where she was going to end up this time. Her nose wrinkled as the rusty smell of dirt wafted towards her. She could feel the sun beating down on her and looked up to see a beautiful blue sky without a single cloud. The warm air was now almost unbearably hot and Stacy was sweating. As she looked down from the clear sky to the rocky, sandy ground, she noticed that she was wearing a pair of brown sandals that she had never seen before.

The bottoms of her new shoes were made from dried leather and were tied around her feet with coarse rope. They didn't protect her feet very well and Stacy could feel rocks pushing up against the soles of her feet. She took a step forward and felt something brush against her legs. She was no longer wearing the jeans and green t-shirt that she had worn to school; instead she had on what looked like a long white robe. The bottom part of her new outfit was a long, loose skirt and it flapped against her legs as she walked. The top of her dress was more like a sheet wrapped around her chest and tied together on her right shoulder. Her left shoulder was bare and Stacy could feel the heat of the sun.

"Where am I?" she wondered aloud.

"In Athens," said a female voice.

"Athens? Where is that?" Stacy said, turning to see a strikingly beautiful woman.

"In Greece. Ancient Greece, actually. You should really pay attention in History."

"I'm in Ancient Greece? Why? And who are you?"

"I'm Athena, the Greek Goddess of Wisdom. Athens is my city. I'm here to show you around and take you to a very special event." Athena was taller than Stacy, but dressed in much the same manner. The only difference was that Athena had gold ties around her waist and her arms were covered with thick, gold bracelets. On her head she wore a golden helmet, and Stacy could see long locks of blonde hair streaming down her back. In her right hand, Athena held a pointy, metal spear and in her left a gold shield. She looked very powerful.

"Athena," breathed Stacy. "I don't understand."

"Don't worry. Stay with me and you'll see how interesting history can be!" Athena took Stacy's hand and started walking with her. As they ambled along, Stacy had a good look around.

She realized that they were standing on a big hill in the middle of a seemingly endless city. There were no people around, and Stacy could see for miles. "This is the Acropolis, Stacy. Do you know what that is?" Stacy knew that she had heard the word before, but she couldn't tell Athena what it meant.

Embarrassed, she shook her head and said, "Not really."

"Almost every Greek city was built on a hill called an acropolis. That way, the people could see if danger was coming and they would know if someone was attacking their city. It was a means of protection."

"I *can* see really far! I guess you would be able to see if the enemy was coming to attack the city."

"That's right; if we are attacked, we can defend the city before it's too late." Stacy could see other, smaller hills in the distance, but mostly she saw the sprawling city laid out below her. It seemed to go on forever.

"How old are you, Athena?" Stacy asked thoughtfully.

"Oh, I'm a lot older than you are."

"We're in Ancient Greece, right?"

"Yes, that's what I said."

"Well, does that mean you're ancient?"

Athena laughed. "Kind of!"

"You're the Goddess of Wisdom?" Stacy watched Athena nod. "Then why do you have a spear and a shield? You look more like a warrior than a genius."

"That's a good question, Stacy. I am also the Goddess of War, but I don't like to fight. I think it's better to use your head in war than to use your weapons."

Stacy was confused. "What do you mean?" she asked.

"Many gods and goddesses come to me for advice before they go to battle. I use my wisdom to help them solve problems without fighting before it comes to war. When I help in times of conflict, I try to be fair and compassionate to all involved. It's better to make both sides happy than to have them destroy each other over their problems."

"That *is* smart!"

"Well, it doesn't always work, but I do everything I can to prevent war before we have to resort to fighting."

Stacy looked around." Where is everyone? There's no one here."

"Well, you're right about that. They're all waiting for us at the special place I am going to take you to."

"What special place? What are you talking about?"

"You'll see!" Athena said with a smile. She pulled on Stacy's arm and began to run. Stacy had no choice but to run with her, as the Greek Goddess was still holding her hand. The cool breeze they created while running felt nice against her hot skin, but Stacy's feet hurt as they pounded on the hard rocks. Suddenly Stacy felt a very strange sensation in her stomach, the same feeling she got when the roller coaster at the fair starts going downhill very fast. "Oh! Athena! What's happening?"

Stacy closed her eyes tightly and didn't open them again until Athena said, "It's okay, Stacy. We're here." Stacy opened her eyes.

"Where's here?" Stacy could see that they were no longer on the Acropolis in Athens. Two rivers were running down a much smaller hill that was covered in thick pine trees. The rivers met at the bottom of the hill where they merged into one bigger, more powerful waterway. The area around the river and hill was almost perfectly flat.

"We're in Olympia. The year is 776 B.C., and you are here to see something very important. Pay attention, Stacy!"

"I will," Stacy promised, wide-eyed. She couldn't believe that the stairs under her bed had led her thousands of years back in time. As Stacy stood there, waiting for the special event to start, she wiped away more sweat from her forehead. "Is it always so hot in Greece?" she asked.

"It is in the summer."

"You still haven't told me where we are!" Stacy complained. "How am I supposed to learn anything if I don't know where we are?"

"I told you - we're in Olympia, Stacy. Be patient. They're about to start."

"What's about to start?" began Stacy, but was cut off by the sound of an enormous, swift procession entering the area in a cloud of dust.

Stacy's open mouth was filled with flying dirt, but she just couldn't manage to get her jaw closed – what she was seeing in front of her was the most amazing thing she had ever seen. She spit out the irony earth and watched four strong, fast brown horses pull a big wooden cart on wheels. Three other carts followed it and they all stopped in the middle of a colossal field. The result was spectacular.

"Those are chariots. This is the start of the event that we have come to see," explained Athena. The men in the chariots were dressed like Stacy and Athena and Stacy found this very funny.

"Why are those men wearing dresses?" Stacy whispered.

"That's how everyone dresses in Ancient Greece, Stacy."

"Even their shoes are the same as mine!" Stacy said, noticing the sandals that the men were wearing.

Stacy thought that her life would be a lot easier if all of her friends dressed the same. Then she wouldn't have to worry about keeping up with the latest fashion and begging her mom to buy her the newest pair of Skechers. Stacy liked fashion and shopping, but she wasn't as crazy about it as some people, like Kimberly. Kimberly always had to have the nicest clothes, dressing like the kids in SMILE and making sure that everyone knew it. Stacy imagined what Kimberly would look like in the long white robes and had to put her hand over her mouth to stop herself from laughing. She glanced up at Athena to see if she had noticed, but the goddess was staring at the action in the middle of the field. They moved closer to get a better look.

"Do you know what's happening?" Athena asked Stacy.

"No, not really. I've never heard of Olympia before. I don't know what happened here." Stacy could see that all along the edge of the flat field were wooden seats. They looked like the bleachers in her school gym, but wobbly and much older. The seats were packed with men, and they, too, were dressed in the white robes. But Stacy couldn't see any women. "Where are the women?" she asked Athena. "I don't see any!"

"That's because they aren't allowed here. You won't see any women or girls at all."

"But what about us? Are we allowed to be here?"

"Oh yes," replied Athena. "We're fine. No one can see us."

"No one can see us?" repeated Stacy in disbelief. "You're kidding!"

"No, I'm not. We're here only to watch and learn - not to participate."

At that moment, a noisy uproar started in the middle of the field where the chariots were sitting. Stacy could hear the men chanting in loud voices, but she couldn't understand what they were saying because they were speaking a different language. The only word Stacy recognized was Zeus. "Zeus!" she exclaimed. "I know that word. Zeus was a Greek God, like you, wasn't he, Athena?" Stacy was pleased that she remembered something from her history lessons.

"He's my father," Athena said, without looking at Stacy.

"Oh!" Stacy said, and then snapped her mouth shut when she realized that she had no idea what to say next.

Athena finally turned to her and said, "Zeus, my father, is the God of the Sky and the ruler of all the Gods. He protects the weak and punishes the wicked. He is the King of all Gods." Athena sounded very proud.

"What are they saying about him?" whispered Stacy.

"This is a festival to honour Zeus, Stacy. There will be races, songs and dances."

"Hm," said Stacy thoughtfully, "that sounds a bit like the Olympics that I watched on TV last year." She finally made the connection. "Olympia! Olympics! Are we at the Olympics, Athena?"

Athena smiled. "Yes, you're right. This is the origin of the Olympic Games."

"Wow! I didn't know they had the Olympics in 776 B.C!" Stacy exclaimed.

"Well, they didn't really start out as the Olympic Games that you're familiar with. This is more of a festival to honour my father. You'll see. Then you can tell me how the Olympics have changed in your time."

Stacy looked up at Athena in awe, "Thank you for bringing me here!"

"You're welcome," Athena said, and the games began.

Athena led Stacy as close to the edge of the field as was possible. "I want you to be able to see everything," she said to Stacy. "You'll learn more if you can see well." Stacy was now close enough to see the sweat on the athletes' faces. About ten men were lining up at the end of the field closest to Stacy and the goddess.

"What country are they from?" Stacy asked Athena.

"Greece, of course!" replied Athena. "All of the athletes are from Greece!"

"Really? All of the athletes in the Olympics are Greek? And men?" Stacy was very surprised. "Nowadays, the athletes come from all over the world. And there are women too! Lots of them. They're really talented!"

"Well, I guess that's one way that things have changed!"

Stacy looked carefully at the men who were competing in the first ever Olympics. They were brown from the sun, but they weren't wearing white robes like all the other Greeks that Stacy had seen. Brown, leathery cloths were tied around their waists, but their chests and legs were left bare. "What are they wearing?" Stacy asked.

"Loincloths. It's what all the athletes wear."

These athletes were all holding a long, pointed wooden pole. Each pole was as tall, or somewhat taller than the man holding it. "Those are javelins," explained Athena. "Each man will have a turn to see who can throw it the farthest." Stacy watched as the first man took his place. He tied a leather strap around the middle of his javelin, and Stacy asked Athena what it was for.

"That's called a thong. The athlete ties it on his javelin to help him get a better grip. It also helps to keep the javelin steady so that it will go farther."

"They don't have those on javelins today," Stacy said. "I know because I saw the javelin throw in the Olympics on TV."

The first athlete was ready, and Stacy gasped as he ran with the javelin in his right hand, holding it close to his head. Before he came to the starting line on the field, he pulled his right hand back, turned his body in the direction of the throw and let go. The javelin hurled over the athlete's head and sailed through the air for some distance before landing.

"That was awesome!" exclaimed Stacy. The next athlete took his place, and Stacy noticed that he tied his thong in a slightly different place than the last. The next four athletes tied their thongs in different places, but most of their javelins went just as far.

"Come here, Stacy," called Athena. "It's time to visit the next event."

"But this one's not over! I want to see who wins!"

"We don't have time to watch all the athletes. You have to get home soon. I want you to see a little more of the other events." As Athena said this, they arrived at another field where more men in the same brown loincloths were lined up ready to run a race. "Running is the oldest form of competition among athletes. There are many strong runners in Ancient Greece. Look how powerful they are!"

Stacy could see the muscles in the runners' legs. They, too, were covered in sweat. "How can they run in this heat? I'm hot just standing here!"

"They're used to it. You're not. They're incredibly swift and can run for a long time. Watch!" Athena said. Stacy heard a loud voice and watched all the runners take off. There were more men running in the race than Stacy had seen throwing the javelins. Athena explained that this was because running was the most important sport and more athletes trained in this area. After the first race was over, the winner was taken into the middle of the field while the crowd stood up and cheered. Another man, dressed in a white robe like Stacy's, put a ribbon in the winner's hair and a crown of leaves on his head.

"What's that?" asked Stacy.

"It's his prize for winning the race. The crown is made from the olive tree."

"That's all he gets for winning?" Stacy asked in disbelief. "Where's his medal?"

"Medal?" asked Athena.

"Yeah, when an athlete wins in our Olympics, they get a medal - like gold, silver or bronze. And they get free stuff from Adidas, Reebok and Nike. They become famous!"

"Nike? Did you say Nike?"

"Yeah. It's a sports company. They make nice clothes and shoes. Do you know of them?"

"No, but I know Nike."

"What?"

"Nike is a Greek Goddess, like me."

"Nike is a Greek Goddess?" Stacy couldn't believe it.

"Sure. She's the Goddess of Victory."

Stacy's attention was drawn back to the field where another race was starting. This race was a bit longer than the first, and Athena explained that there were many races of different lengths. The winner was again presented with his crown and ribbon, and Stacy watched while the hot, sweaty, dust covered athletes rubbed oil all over their bodies. "What's that for?" she asked, watching as the athletes scraped the oil off their bodies.

"That's how they clean themselves. They're all sweaty and dusty, but there isn't a lot of water here in the summer. The oil takes the sweat and dirt off." Stacy didn't think that she would like this method of cleaning. She made a mental note to appreciate the next bath that she took.

Over to the other side of the field Stacy could hear more loud voices. Athena led her in that direction, and as they got closer, Stacy could hear singing. Stacy enjoyed watching the men singing and dancing, even though she couldn't understand what they were saying. "What's this?" she asked Athena.

"These festivals include a lot of singing and dancing. Remember, it's a celebration to honour Zeus, not just an athletic competition."

"There isn't a lot of singing and dancing nowadays," said Stacy. "Except maybe at the beginning and the end."

"Okay, there's time for at least one more event before I send you home."

"No, I don't want to go home! I want to stay in Greece with you!"

"That's not possible, Stacy. Come over here. The discus throw is starting."

On this field were five more athletes, all holding a piece of stone, shaped like a flying saucer. The stones looked dreadfully heavy. Each athlete took a turn throwing his discus and Stacy gazed in wonder. The athlete held the discus in his hand and started swinging it up and down. As it got higher, the athlete's other hand would come up to give it extra support. When he was finally ready, he used the motion of the swing to hurl the discus as far as it would go. But before all the athletes had their turn, Athena was dragging Stacy to the next event.

"Athena! I can't run that fast. I'm too hot!" Stacy whined as she wiped sweat from her forehead.

"There's not much time left, Stacy."

"What are we going to see now?" Stacy panted as she hurried to keep up with the goddess.

"Jumping is another important event, like running, because it's essential when fighting a war."

"Huh? What does jumping have to do with war?"

"The Greek countryside is filled with holes and ravines. The soldiers have to be able to run and jump over them so they can move faster in battles." Stacy couldn't believe how wise Athena was, and how much she had already taught her.

Stacy saw the jumpers lined up next to a shallow pit. They held large stones in their hands and Stacy had to ask Athena what they were for. "They're weights. They help the jumpers to jump even farther."

"How? Jumpers in our time don't carry stones."

"Watch. You'll see!"

The first jumper took his place and started to run toward the pit. He was swinging his weights back and forth before he took his jump. Just before he was about to land, he threw the weights backward and even Stacy could see that this motion helped to propel him farther.

"Amazing!" Stacy said to herself. She turned to look for Athena, and was startled to see her walking away from the field. "Athena! Wait!" called Stacy, running after her. "Where are you going?"

"Follow me, Stacy. It's time!"

"What? No! I'm not going home. I want to stay here with you until the Olympics are over. I love Ancient Greece!"

"The festival will go on for days. You can't see it all. I'm sorry."

Stacy stomped her feet in anger and was surprised when she heard thumping. She looked down and saw that she was once again wearing her Skechers, which were banging on the wooden steps leading back to her bedroom.

Stacy wiped a tear from her check and climbed back up to her room. As she put the trap door down, she whispered, "Bye, Athena. Thank you! Please say Hello to Zeus. And Nike!"

After she had moved her bed back into place, Stacy went downstairs to see her mom. She didn't feel like being alone. "Hi, Mom!"

"Hi, Stacy. What were you doing? You've been up in your room for a long time!"

"I was just reading a book."

"Oh, about what?"

"Um, Ancient Greece. We're learning about it in History."

"Well, that sounds interesting. But I thought you didn't like History very much."

"I don't, but Ancient Greece is really cool."

"Look at me!" Stacy's mom said, with a frown.

"Why? What's wrong?"

"Your nose is all red. It almost looks like you have a sunburn!"

"No! It's uh… it's probably just from keeping my nose in my book too long," Stacy said, with a laugh. "I'm tired. Good night, Mom!" she said, kissing her mom and running up to her room to check out her red nose.

CHAPTER EIGHT

S tacy woke up the next morning with a gasp. *Was it true?* she thought. *Did I really go to Ancient Greece?* She was almost looking forward to history class that day, but the thought of seeing Jade and Kimberly put her in a bad mood before she even stepped out of bed. *I wish I could just spend the rest of my life at the bottom of my stairs. I'm always happy down there with my good friends, Athena, SMILE and Amanda. My real life sucks.*

"Stacy! Are you up?" she heard her mother yell, and knew she'd better get dressed. A quick look in the mirror told her that her nose was still red, but not as red as it had been last night. It had actually stung when she put lotion on it before going to bed!

When they arrived at school, Stacy sighed before she got out of the car. "Do I have to go to school today?" she asked her mom, even though she knew the answer.

"Of course! You're already behind in Math and you don't want to miss History now that you're enjoying the topic so much! Don't be silly! Go on!"

"Bye, Mom." Stacy sighed as she slammed the car door shut.

By the time math class came around, Stacy was too happy to let three wrong answers get her down. She had really shone in history class. Her teacher had asked them to name the date of the very first Olympics and Stacy's hand had been the first one up. "The Olympics started in 776 B.C., but they weren't really the same as our Olympics. They were more of a festival, to honour Zeus, who was King of the Gods."

"Very good, Stacy! Well done. That's absolutely right! Now, who knows which events were part of the ancient Olympics?" asked Miss Terrence.

Stacy's hand was the only one that went up, so Miss Terrence had no choice but to call on her again. "Running was the most important sport so there were lots of races. Jumping was important too because the Greeks had to jump over holes during war. There were no women allowed at the games, but the men threw things like the javelin and discus." Stacy could tell that her teacher and her classmates were very impressed.

Afterwards, Jade came up to her. "That was great, Stacy! How did you know all that stuff?"

"I ..." Stacy started, but was cut off when Kimberly came and pulled Jade away.

"We don't want to hear any more about Ancient Greece from her, do we Jade?" said Kimberly, as she pulled Jade away. Jade threw Stacy a quick smile, but Stacy didn't think that Jade saw her smile back before Kim dragged her off.

During lunch, Stacy told Trinh, Christina and Lacey everything else that she had learned the previous night. They were intrigued, and Lacey wanted to know if she could borrow the book that Stacy had read. "Um, I think my dad has to take it back to the library tonight, but I'll see," she lied.

After school, Stacy went straight home to finish her homework. All she had to do that night were some history questions and she flew through them. When she came down for dinner, she was smiling. "What's got you so pleased with yourself?" asked her mom.

"I'm done my homework already, and it was fun!"

"Really? I guess you didn't have any math homework today, then."

"Nope. Just history questions."

"Well, I'm glad to see that you are enjoying something."

"It's easy to enjoy a subject when you're good at it!"

Stacy's mom just looked at her and smiled. "I guess so!"

During dinner Stacy told her family even more about the first Olympics. Mr. Myers was completely impressed that she knew about the stones that the jumpers had used. "I was on my track and field team in high school, you know," he said.

"Really? Were you any good?" asked Stacy.

"I wasn't the best on the team, but I wasn't the worst either. Maybe if I had some rocks in my hands I could have jumped farther!" Everyone laughed. "Running was my best event. I was fast! So fast that on a good day, you couldn't even see me! If you blinked, you'd miss me!"

"Really?" asked Danny, wide-eyed.

"Dad!" groaned Stacy. "Don't be silly!" She turned to her brother. "Yeah, Danny, he ran so fast he could catch Superman!" Stacy joked. "See if you can catch me, Dad! I'm done!" Stacy pushed her chair from the table and started stacking the dishes. When she was finished, she went back up to her room and moved her bed away to reveal the trap door for the fifth time.

Stacy was so accustomed to going down through the trap door that she didn't get nervous anymore. She marched down the stairs, anxious for her next adventure to begin, and soon enough, Stacy could tell that things were starting to change. She could smell the sweet scent of vanilla. Stacy couldn't hear her feet stomping on the wooden steps anymore, and when she looked down she saw that the floor she was now standing on was covered with thick, white carpet. The walls were painted a light shade of pink and she soon realized that she was in a bedroom in someone's house. She didn't know whose house it was, but she was sure that she had never been here before.

Stacy decided to have a quick look around to see if she could find anything that would reveal where she was. A king-sized bed stood against the far wall in the centre of the large room, covered with the whitest, fluffiest comforter that Stacy had ever seen. Lacy frills hung down the sides and pink heart shaped pillows were scattered around the head of the bed, perfectly matching the walls. Beside the bed stood a small, tidy, white table, with a clock and a pink lamp on top of it. A vanilla air freshener explained the sweet smell. A white dresser with gold handles stood against another wall and Stacy went over to see what was on it.

A ballerina figurine, a music box with a figure skater on top, and a framed picture were all she could see. Stacy thought about her own dresser at home and how it was always cluttered with knick-knacks. She picked up the picture frame and almost dropped it when she realized whose room she was in. The silver frame held a photo of Kimberly, wearing one of her ballet costumes, with a big smile plastered on her face. She put the picture back down and looked in the mirror above the dresser. Stacy was shocked to find that she couldn't see herself. She blinked her eyes, looked again, but she still couldn't see her own reflection. She reached a hand toward the mirror and tapped on the glass. There was no sound.

From outside of the room came a sudden loud crash and a lot of yelling. Stacy looked around in panic. She wasn't supposed to be here! What if Kimberly came in and found Stacy in her room? That probably wouldn't go over too well. Stacy looked around for a hiding place, but it was too late. Kimberly came running through the door in a whirlwind and flung herself down on the bed. Stacy could see that she was upset about something and watched as big tears rolled down Kimberly's cheeks. Her chest heaved as she inhaled a big breath and let out a sob.

"Um, Kimberly?" said Stacy, softly. There was no reply. In fact it didn't look as if Kimberly was aware of Stacy's presence. Stacy cleared her throat and tried again. Kimberly was really crying now. She looked as if though she might never stop. "Kimberly?" said Stacy. She was sure that she was speaking as loudly as she could, but Stacy couldn't even hear her own voice.

Timidly, she tiptoed over and tapped Kimberly on the shoulder. There was no response at all. Stacy quickly understood that she was invisible to Kimberly, but she wasn't sure what to do. She felt awkward standing in Kimberly's room and watching her cry.

Kimberly must have come straight from ballet class because she was wearing her white tights and pink body suit. Her slippers were still in her hand and just as her mother walked in, Kimberly abruptly sat up and threw them across the room. Stacy thought about hiding again, but Kimberly's mother didn't seem to be able to see her either.

"What do you think you're doing, young lady?" Kimberly's mom asked, simultaneously picking up the slippers and smoothing her long black skirt. "That's no way to treat your things!"

"I don't care! I hate them! I hate ballet! And I hate you for making me go!" Kimberly screamed with another loud sob. Stacy watched in awe from the corner of the room.

"Don't you dare talk to me that way! What's the problem? Why do you hate ballet all of a sudden?" Kimberly's mom said, taking off her pointy, black high-heeled shoes and rubbing her feet.

"I've always hated it!"

"No you haven't! You love your ballet classes!"

"No, I don't! That's just what you think. You love them! You love to watch me do my ballet, but I don't like it!"

"Kimberly," started her mom, but by this time Kimberly had jumped off the bed and started undoing the bun that was holding up her long, blonde hair.

"Don't you get it, Mom? Every day after school I have to go straight to ballet! Or gymnastics! Or flute lessons! It's always something!"

"Yes, but it's good for you. Think of all the opportunities you have! None of your other friends get to do extra activities like you!"

"Yes, they do! Jade takes a dance class, but only twice a

week! She doesn't have to get up early every morning and go skating before school. She doesn't have to go to lessons every day after school, and then come home to do her homework! I don't have time for fun! I hate it!"

Stacy was shocked to hear Kimberly talk to her mother like that, and shocked to learn that she hated all of her activities. She always bragged about them at school.

"I don't have time for this now, Kimberly," her mother said. "I have to get ready for my meeting tonight."

"You have a meeting tonight? Again?"

"Yes, but you'll be fine. Sandra is coming over to baby-sit you. If you get your homework done in time, the two of you can make some popcorn and watch a movie."

"I don't want to watch a movie with her! I..." Kimberly held back a sob. "Why do you have to go? You're never home anymore! Dad's been in Europe for two weeks now and the only person I ever see is Sandra."

"I can't do anything about it, Kimberly. My job is important. Do your homework and come down for dinner in half an hour." Her mom walked out and stiffly closed the door behind her.

"I'm important," Kimberly whispered to herself as she got out her history book.

But instead of starting the assignment, she just looked at the pages and cried. Finally she picked up her pencil and started answering the questions in her notebook.

Stacy could see that Kimberly was having a lot of trouble. She kept flipping through the textbook searching for the information she needed to answer the questions correctly. *But the questions were so easy*, thought Stacy, confused. *Kimberly's much smarter than I am, why is she having such a hard time with it? I thought she knew everything.*

After struggling with her history homework for half an hour, Kimberly finally gave up, pulled a pair of sweat pants over her tights, and headed down for dinner. Stacy followed her out the room and down a long hallway, amazed by all the paintings hanging on the walls. Some were portraits, but most of the paintings showed beautiful scenery, like beaches and mountains. A very old looking wooden table sat at the end of the long hallway and on top of it was a tall, crystal vase filled with fresh, orange flowers.

Stacy followed Kimberly down the stairs and hoped that when they arrived at the bottom, she would automatically be transported back to her own house. But there was no such luck. It looked like she would be watching Kimberly eat dinner with her mom.

"Well, I see you've stopped crying," her mom said while Kimberly washed her hands at the sink. "Have you finished your homework?" Kimberly's mom had changed out of her matching suit jacket, and was now wearing a green sweater with her black skirt.

"Yes." Kimberly sat down at the big glass table in the middle of the pristine kitchen.

"Okay, then let's hurry up and eat so I can get to my meeting." Stacy watched Kimberly's eyes fill up with tears again, but Kimberly blinked them away before her mom noticed.

"Will you be home tomorrow night?" Kimberly asked tentatively.

"I'm not sure. It depends how this meeting goes tonight."

"If you're home, can we watch a movie together tomorrow?"

Kimberly's mom stopped and smiled. "Of course. I know I haven't been home that much but work has been really busy. Dad will be home on the weekend and we'll go to the zoo together on Sunday, okay?"

Stacy saw Kimberly smile for the first time that night. "Promise?"

"Promise!"

Stacy watched as they ate their chicken, peas and rice, and was struck by how different Kimberly's family was from her own. At dinnertime in Stacy's house, her family talked and laughed together, but Kimberly and her mom hardly said a

word to each other. Stacy wandered over to look at the refrig-
erator to see what was pinned up on it. The Myers' fridge was
always plastered with Stacy's and Danny's work for everyone
to see. Kimberly's fridge only had two pieces of paper pinned
up with magnets, and they both looked like adult papers from
her mom's work.

After dinner was over, Sandra arrived and Kimberly's mom
left for her meeting. "Hi, Kim," said Sandra, who looked to be
about sixteen years old and had big red streaks in her black
hair. She was wearing jeans and a black t-shirt that sported the
name of a band Stacy had never heard of before. "What do you
want to do tonight?"

"Nothing much. I have a book to read. I think I'll just do
that and then go to bed early. I had a hard ballet lesson today."
Kimberly looked sad again.

"You don't want to invite any of your friends over? I don't
mind. We could all play a game or something." They walked
into the living room and Stacy followed.

"Um, no. I think I'll just read." Stacy felt like she was walking into a movie set as she entered the huge living room. Three
brown leather couches formed a semi circle in the middle of the
room, and the hardwood floor was covered in beautiful ma-
roon and blue carpets. One whole wall consisted of windows,
and the other wall was full of electronic equipment. Stacy had
only ever seen a TV that size in an electronics store.

"I've never met any of your friends, Kim. How come they
never come over?"

"My mom doesn't really like them to come over during the
week. I have homework and stuff to do," Kimberly said to
Sandra, but to herself mumbled, *because I don't really have any.*

"Not even that Jade you talk about all the time? She sounds
nice."

"Oh, she is," Kimberly smiled again. "But I think she's mad
at me today." With this statement, Stacy's ears perked up.

"Really? Why?"

"Today in History I made fun of her friend, Stacy. I don't

think Stacy likes me."

"Why not?"

"I don't know. But Stacy's not speaking to Jade because she's friends with me and Jade misses Stacy. I don't see why – she has me now!" Stacy didn't like that comment one bit, but she was very happy to hear Kimberly say that Jade missed her.

Kimberly trudged back up the stairs to her room and Stacy followed. When Stacy got to the top and still hadn't been transported to her own house, she went back down the stairs and tried one more time. Nothing. *I guess it isn't time for me to leave yet*, she thought, and walked down the hall to see what Kimberly was up to. She had changed into a pair of pink pyjamas and was in bed with a book. A big, white teddy bear was perched on her lap, and Kimberly was talking to it. "My mom and dad might not be here, but I do have you. And Jade. I won't be lonely anymore. Jade really is my friend, even if no one else is." Kimberly brushed away a single tear, turned off the light and rolled over.

With a strange feeling in the pit of her stomach, Stacy watched Kimberly get comfortable in her bed. She wasn't sure what that strange feeling was, but she thought that it might actually be sympathy. Stacy sauntered out into the hallway, down the stairs and found herself at the bottom of the wooden steps leading into her room.

She climbed up, put her bed back and went to find Danny. She had never been so glad to have a brother before; it would be awfully lonely without him around, annoying as he could be sometimes. She knew what it was like when her dad went on business trips, even if it was only for a few days and not weeks. At least and Danny and Stacy had each other for company. Stacy loved her family, and had never felt as lonely in her own home as Kimberly did.

I thought Kimberly had tons of friends, thought Stacy. *Maybe that's just at school where everyone wants to hang out with her. It doesn't sound like she has time for friends outside of school.* Stacy thought about how lonely Kimberly must be. *Maybe I should try to be nicer to her*, she thought. Now that she had seen that Kimberly wasn't so perfect after all, she didn't seem to dislike her as much.

Stacy went to bed that night with a resolution to befriend Kimberly the next day. She was both nervous and excited, but she knew she had to try. After all, if Jade seemed to like Kimberly so much, she had to be worth the effort.

CHAPTER NINE

Wednesday before school, Stacy waited bravely in the parking lot for Jade and Kimberly to arrive. Before falling asleep the night before, Stacy had promised herself that she would talk to the two girls first thing in the morning. She might have made a mess of things with Jade, but she could try and make it right, and maybe even make a new friend in the process.

Soon enough, Kimberly's car arrived and the two girls got out. Kimberly's eyes looked raw and Stacy remembered how she had been crying the night before. "Jade! Kimberly!" Stacy called, running over to them.

"What do you want?" Kimberly said, glaring at Stacy.

"Uh, nothing." Stacy didn't know what to say. She had just wanted to show Kimberly that she liked her, and wasn't expecting Kimberly to be so cruel in return. The three girls just stared at each other.

"Hi, Stacy," Jade said awkwardly. "Did you finish your homework?"

"Yes, it was easy!" Stacy said, happy that Jade was speaking to her. "Did you?"

"Yeah. I like learning about Ancient Greece. I just hope that we don't have too much homework today. SMILE is on MTV tonight and I have to watch!"

"Ooh! What time?"

"Jade, let's go," Kimberly was tugging on Jade's arm.

"Are you going to watch SMILE tonight, Kimberly?" Stacy asked her, trying again to be nice.

"No, I don't have time for stupid stuff like that. I have a flute lesson so I'll be busy practicing. Maybe you could do something more useful too, like doing your math homework for once!"

"What? I do my homework every night!"

"Yeah. You just don't do it right," Kimberly said, throwing her head back and laughing.

Stacy didn't say anything in reply to Kimberly. Instead, she stormed off and ignored Jade, who was calling her name. *I tried*, she thought. *And now I know why she doesn't have any other friends.* But Stacy couldn't figure out why she still felt sorry for Kimberly, and why Jade continued to be her friend.

Sure enough, during math class, Stacy was called on to answer a question and got it wrong. She could hear Kimberly giggling at the back of the room, and turned around to give her a nasty look, but stopped when she saw Jade poking Kimberly. The whole class heard Jade say to Kimberly, "Leave her alone!" Stacy forgot all about her embarrassment at the wrong answer she had given, and smiled when she heard Jade sticking up for her.

After school Jade rushed after Stacy and finally caught up with her. "Where's Kimberly?" Stacy asked her.

"I don't know. I wanted to talk to you."

"Won't Kimberly be mad at you?"

"Stacy…"

"I'm sorry, Jade, but she's not very nice, is she? I really want to be your friend again, but how can I be if you're always with her?"

"I know, but you have to give her a chance! She really can be nice."

"I gave her a chance this morning. Now it's her turn to be nice." Stacy waited for Jade to say something, anything, like – *Okay, forget about Kimberly! I don't need her; you're my best friend!*

But Jade just stood there with her head down, kicking at an invisible stone on the pavement. So Stacy headed home, alone.

When she rounded the corner to her house, she was surprised to see her dad's car in the driveway. "Dad?" she called, opening the door.

"In here!" he called from the kitchen.

"How come you're home so early?"

"I left a little early so I could see my favourite daughter!"

"Your favourite daughter? Who's that? Do I know her?" Stacy joked.

"You not only know her, but you are her!" Stacy's dad gave her a big hug.

"I love you, Dad. I'm glad you're home early."

"So, what do you want to do?"

What Stacy really wanted to do was go for a bike ride, go swimming, watch TV or challenge her dad to a game on the Wii. But there was one thing that had to be done before they could have any fun. "I have lots of math homework, Dad. I better do that first."

"All right. Why don't I help you, and then we can go for a bike ride?"

"Really? You'll help me?"

"Help you, yes. But don't expect me to give you the answers."

"Please, Dad! Then we can go for a bike ride sooner!"

"You need to be able to solve the problems on your own. Go get your books. The sooner we get started, the sooner we can go."

It took Stacy less than half an hour to do her homework after her dad went over it with her. Homework out of the way, they were able to enjoy a long bike ride. When they returned home, dinner smells greeted their noses and they went into the kitchen to see what was cooking.

"Yum! Tacos!" Stacy said.

"Hope you're hungry! There's a lot here!" Mrs. Myers teased.

"We worked up a good appetite on our bike ride!" Mr. Myers laughed. "Let's go get washed up and then we can eat!"

During dinner Stacy and her dad related the details of the bike ride they had taken earlier. Stacy's dad had almost run over a squirrel. Luckily, he'd put on his brakes in time and the squirrel was saved, but Mr. Myers fell off his bike when it stopped so abruptly. As Stacy watched her family laughing and eating together, she was reminded of the quiet, lonely dinner she had witnessed Kimberly share with her mom yesterday. *It still doesn't give her the right to be mean*, Stacy thought.

After dinner, Stacy did what she had done almost every night for the past week - went up to her room, moved her bed and opened the trap door. She closed her eyes and marched down the steps determinedly. She promised herself that she wouldn't open them until she knew that she had begun her next adventure. But because her eyes were closed, she couldn't see, and around the fourth step, she tripped and went sprawling down the remainder of the stairs. Stacy braced herself for the hard landing, but surprisingly, she didn't feel any pain. She felt quite light and once she had landed, she tilted her head upwards and slowly opened her eyes.

She was greeted by a plethora of green; so much green in fact, that Stacy thought perhaps she had fallen into a bowl of broccoli soup, or a big bag of grass. *This doesn't look too promising*, she thought to herself. Stacy shook her head to clear her eyes and heard a strange whooshing sound. She tried to reach up and rub her eyes, but she was confronted with a very strange problem.

She had no arms! Or hands, or fingers! What Stacy saw when she looked down caused her to let out an audible gasp. Except it wasn't really a gasp, but more of a squeaky croak. For Stacy wasn't Stacy anymore, she was a bird.

Stacy had been frightened enough when she found herself in Ancient Greece wearing strange clothes. But to find herself in a completely different body was almost too much for Stacy and she began to cry. Big, soggy tears dripped from her beady, black eyes onto the white feathers surrounding them. Two or three tears were big enough to roll right off the white feathers and make their way down Stacy's pointy, black beak before splashing onto the ground.

Another tear rolled all the way down Stacy's neck and nestled into the vibrant, red feathers that covered her neck and back. She took one of her wings and attempted to brush the last tear away, but she couldn't bend the long, yellow and blue feathers towards her eyes. Her sharp, black talons clenched against the ground as she took a deep breath (she could still do that) and decided that she had better stop being a baby and get on with the adventure. She was learning just to accept whatever happened when she ventured down the stairs.

She could smell wet vegetation as the warm air swirled around her face. Stacy started walking along the uneven ground, which was difficult to do with the long, red feathers of her tail dragging along behind her. "I'm a parrot, aren't I?" she said to no one in particular, but hoping that someone, or something, would respond. *Where do parrots live?* she thought to herself. "The rainforest!" she remembered. *But why am I here? I already know about the rainforest, we studied it in Grade Four.*

"Yes, that's right," she heard from her left and looked over. "You're in the rainforest." Standing on a big, grey boulder was another colourful bird, about the same size as Stacy.

"Are you a toucan?" she asked.

"You're awfully quick today," replied the bird.

"A talking toucan. That's strange."

"You're a talking parrot yourself. What's so weird about a talking toucan?" Stacy had forgotten that she was a bird. Not just any bird though, a beautiful bird, like the toucan she was talking to. His black body was shiny and clean.

"Do you have a name?" Stacy asked the toucan, looking carefully at the spot where his black feathers met light yellow feathers to cover the bottom of his neck. Feathers of pure orange surrounded his eyes and Stacy was reminded of a favourite sweater she'd had as a toddler.

"No, not really. We don't use names in the rainforest. What are you looking at?"

Stacy couldn't help but notice the toucan's exquisite beak. The long, thick bill started off in a light shade of orange and gradually darkened into red. Stacy could even see flecks of yellow in some parts. It looked like a mini rainbow sticking out from his head. "I, uh, I just think that your beak is really beautiful."

"Thank you," said the toucan, flying off, his short, black tail feathers flapping in the air.

"Wait!" cried Stacy. "Don't leave me!"

"Well, come on then. I don't have all day, you know!" he said, looking back at Stacy.

"All day for what?" she inquired, straining to lift herself off the ground.

"To show you around the rainforest. There's a lot to learn here."

Stacy was beginning to the think that everyone thought that she was brainless. "I know a lot about the rainforest already! Really! I studied it in school last year." *Come on, give me a break*, she thought.

"Yes, but have you ever been in one?"

"Well, no," she admitted.

"There's the difference. You'll see." The toucan observed Stacy jumping off the ground and landing right back on her talons without getting anywhere near taking off. He turned around and flew back to help her. "What's wrong?"

"I can't fly. I'll never keep up with you."

"You're a parrot! Of course you can fly!"

"No, actually, I'm a little girl, and little girls can't fly!" she said, angrily.

"You think you're a little girl. Forget about that. You have to believe you are a parrot!"

"Hrumph," Stacy mumbled and tried her hardest to forget who she was. She closed her eyes and imagined flying effortlessly over the canopy of the rainforest, looking for food. She tentatively jumped up and came right back down. No matter how hard she focused, she still couldn't fly.

"Don't jump! Glide! Use your wings!" Without opening her eyes, Stacy extended her wings out to the side and flapped them up and down very slowly. Nothing.

"That's better! Try again!" encouraged the toucan. Stacy took a deep breath, pushed all little girl thoughts out of her mind and flapped her wings, once, twice and finally three times. She felt her feet leave the ground and her stomach drop. She was flying! If only she'd remembered to open her eyes...Stacy flew into a tall tree and fell right back down to the ground.

"I'm not having very much fun in the rainforest!" she yelled. "I want to go home! I haven't learned anything here, except how to hit my head on a tree!"

"Relax. You've learned how to fly; now you just have to learn how to open your eyes. Flying with your eyes closed isn't very smart."

"I know!" Stacy admitted sheepishly. I was concentrating so hard, I just kind of forgot."

"Well, let's try it one more time. If you keep your eyes open, I'm positive that you'll be fine. Ready?"

"I'll try one more time. If I don't make it, then can I go home?"

"Deal. But I know you'll make it this time."

Stacy took her place far away from the tree she had just flown into, and opened her eyes as wide as they would go. She flapped her wings and rose into the air immediately. "Wow! I'm doing it!" She hung there for a few seconds, only a few feet off the ground, while she caught her breath. Then she flapped her wings again, harder this time, and flew even higher. Her stomach didn't feel funny this time because her eyes were open and she could see where she was going. She wasn't going very fast, just fast enough to catch up with the toucan, who was flying ahead of her. Stacy felt light and airy.

The toucan started flying higher and Stacy felt butterflies in her belly. "Don't go so high! I like it down here!"

"You can't see anything from down there and the trees will get in your way. Come up here. If you're still scared, we can land on a treetop." Stacy didn't like the sound of that, but the toucan was soaring so high that she could hardly see him. She aimed for a break in the trees and flapped her wings harder and harder. She glided upwards easily and was relieved to see the toucan sitting on a branch at the top of the forest canopy.

"That wasn't so bad, was it?"

"Yes, it was! I'm still shaking."

"Relax. You did fine. Once you learn to fly, you can't forget. It's like riding a bike!"

"What? What do you know about riding bikes?" Stacy said to the toucan, but he was already flying off. She easily pushed off the branch to follow him, without even thinking about what she was doing. The scenery below her was so amazing that she almost forgot to flap her wings and started plunging downwards. The rainforest canopy was so thick that Stacy was pretty sure she wouldn't hurt herself even if she did plummet down.

She could see several trees sticking out above the canopy and flew over to one to have a rest. Stacy knew from school that these tall trees formed the emergent layer of the rainforest. They stuck out just a bit farther than the thick canopy. "Can we go back down now? It's lovely up here, but I'd like to see some animals and plants up close."

"No problem! Follow me." The toucan found a tiny opening in the canopy and Stacy followed him through, right into the heart of the rainforest.

He landed in a clearing and Stacy set down beside him. "Careful!" said the toucan.

"What?"

"You almost landed on that frog."

"What frog?"

"That one right there," he said, pointing to a tiny speck of red.

"That's a frog?" Stacy was flabbergasted. The frog was shorter than her baby finger and she wouldn't have seen it if the toucan hadn't pointed it out to her. She moved in for a closer look, but again, the toucan warned her.

"It's a Poison Dart Frog. Don't get too close!"

"Poison?"

"Yes, poison. Not all of them are dangerous, but some have chemicals under their skin that can really hurt you." Stacy gaped as the miniscule frog hopped amongst the leaves covering the forest floor.

"Do they live in the leaf litter?" Stacy asked.

"Yes, they stay mostly on the forest floor, but sometimes they hop onto logs. They can't go much higher than that."

Stacy followed the frog, keeping her distance. She could see that the top of its head and body were bright red, but as she got closer, she noticed that its legs were mainly black. White lines formed attaching circles that reminded Stacy of leopard spots. Its four feet only had three long, whitish, skinny toes each. "It's beautiful!" she breathed, but her whisper frightened the poison dart frog; it hopped away so hastily that Stacy couldn't even see in which direction the amphibian had gone. "I lost it!"

"It's okay. There's plenty more to look at. What would you like to see?"

"Nothing else poisonous. Oh! Look at that tree! It has a strangler vine." Stacy flew over to a tall tree that reached all the way up to the canopy. Its roots were so monstrous and sticking so far out of the ground that Stacy almost flew into one of them. She landed on a branch halfway up and inspected the strangler vine. The vine started at the very bottom of the tree and wrapped itself around the tree's thick trunk. As it got higher up, the vine got thicker and branched off in several directions. "The strangler vine is going to kill this tree, isn't it?"

"Yes, I'm afraid you're right. It will take a long time, but eventually the vine will make its way to the top of the tree and strangle it. The tree will die."

"Can we help it?" Stacy felt sorry for the tree.

"We could, but that would mean we'd have to kill the strangler vine. It's best not to upset the delicate balance of the rainforest."

"I guess, but I'm sad that the tree will die."

"Me too."

The toucan flew off and Stacy patted the tree softly with her wing before following him. He flew to a smaller tree that was only half as tall as the one with the strangler vine. "This is the middle layer of the rainforest, and we'll see things here that you won't see in the other layers," he said.

"Geckos! I think geckos live in the middle layer. Do you know any?"

"I don't know every animal in the rainforest, but I am sure if we look hard enough we can find a gecko or two." Stacy strained her eyes to see if she could spot any movement. She knew that green geckos would be hard to find on the green trees. The middle layer of the rainforest was comparatively dark because the thick trees of the canopy prevented too much light from getting through.

After a minute or two of silent staring, Stacy saw movement out of the corner of her left eye. She looked at the toucan, who was nodding in the direction of the motion. Stacy slowly turned her head and searched for the small lizard. It was hard to see, but Stacy knew where to look. The gecko was no bigger than Danny's hand and it was moving slowly along a branch of the next tree. It was a little lighter than the green of the tree's leaves and the moss on the branch, but dark flecks on its back made it easy for Stacy to spot.

"How does it move so easily? I'd fall right out of the tree!" Stacy whispered.

"It has suction cups on its feet. They help it grip the tree so it doesn't fall out."

"It has more toes than the poison dart frog. The gecko has five – just like me!" She looked down at her talons and added, "Well, usually." It was so easy to forget that she was a parrot here in the rainforest.

"Katydid!" shouted the toucan suddenly, and Stacy watched in dismay as the gecko darted away.

"Katy did what?" Stacy asked, confused. "I thought you said there were no names in the rainforest. Who's Katy?"

The toucan laughed. "A katydid is a rainforest insect. I thought you studied the rainforest." The look on the toucan's face reminded Stacy of her math teacher.

"Well, I did, but we mostly learned about the different levels of the rainforest. We studied some of the things that live here, like monkeys, and jaguars and birds and butterflies and scorpions and...," Stacy paused. "I did learn a lot, but I guess I still have a lot more to learn, don't I?"

"Oh yes, there are thousands of living things in a rainforest. Can you see the katydid?" Stacy stared hard at the branch in front of her where the toucan was pointing.

"No! I don't know what I am looking for."

"You'll have to look closely. Katydids are masters of disguise."

"What do you mean?"

"They can camouflage themselves so their enemies can't see them and eat them. This one looks like a sick leaf."

"You mean that?" Stacy said, pointing at a wilting, brown speckled leaf.

"Yes! That's it!"

"But it looks just like a dead leaf."

"Exactly. That's so other insects will think it's just a diseased leaf. Insects and animals will only eat healthy leaves, so the katydid is safe."

"It still just looks like a leaf to me." Stacy looked really hard, and she was able to pick out two long sticks that the toucan said were the katydid's antennae.

"There are lots of different kinds of katydids in the forest. I saw a pink one once, but those are rare. Do you want to look for more?"

"Yeah! You mean they don't all look like leaves?"

"Oh, no. You'll see. Follow me." Stacy flew off after the toucan. She was starting to like this method of traveling; it was easy, fast and free!

The toucan flew just under the middle level of the rainforest. "There are fewer things to fly into here," he said to Stacy. A few minutes later, he landed on a small branch close to the forest floor. It belonged to another tall tree that reached all the way up to the canopy. The branch was covered in thick green moss, which felt nice and soft under Stacy's talons. She looked over to the toucan who was pointing to a spot on the branch only a few feet away from where Stacy was sitting.

This time Stacy spotted the katydid easily. It resembled a grasshopper, but a lot more colourful. It looked nothing like the last katydid that Stacy had seen - or tried to see. "This is a Rainbow Katydid," the toucan explained. Its long, skinny body was bright green, and its small, yellow head had two antennae sticking out of it. This katydid had four stick-like legs covered in thick stripes of yellow and blue, ending in red feet.

"But if it's so colourful, won't its enemies be able to find it and eat it? This one isn't camouflaged very well."

"The bright colours serve as a warning to the enemies. It scares them off."

Stacy felt something tickle her right talon and looked down to see what it was. What she saw looked like another peculiar grasshopper and she knew right away that it must be a katydid. She didn't want to say anything and scare it away, so she examined it closely without alerting the toucan.

It was closer to her than any other living thing she had encountered in the rainforest so far. This katydid had a short, fatter body with the same antennae protruding out from its head. But what made it look so strange were its legs. Two long limbs stuck straight out from its sides, almost like the wings of an airplane. The insect was largely brown, with a few lighter spots.

"That's an Airplane Katydid," the toucan whispered, letting Stacy know that he had noticed it too.

"It does look just like an airplane!" The talking scared off the insect, and Stacy got one last glimpse of it before it disappeared into the camouflage of the tree.

"I have one more thing to show you," the toucan said to

Stacy. "Follow me!" As Stacy flew along, she knew that it must be almost time for her to go. She looked down and tried to memorize everything that she was seeing. The toucan swooped quickly to the left, and when Stacy followed she could see something that she hadn't yet seen in the rainforest. A swift, wide river lay just ahead and that's where the toucan was headed.

He landed on a gigantic boulder by the river's edge. "Here you go," he said as Stacy set down beside him. "It's time for you to leave now."

By now, Stacy knew better than to argue. "Okay. I had a great time flying with you! Thank you for teaching me so much."

"You're welcome."

"How do I get home?"

"The river. Just jump in."

"But I'm a bird! Birds don't swim."

"You're a little girl, not a bird."

"What?" Stacy looked down at herself and was surprised to find that she had turned back into her normal self. She smiled. "Just jump in?"

"Yes. That's all."

"But, aren't there things in there that can hurt me?"

"No. There might be some water bugs and a catfish or two, but they'll leave you alone."

Stacy took a deep breath, said, "Good-bye!" and jumped in. She didn't feel the water, she didn't get the slightest bit wet and she wasn't at all scared - for when she landed, she landed right at the bottom of the stairs. She was home.

After putting her room back in order, Stacy sat on her bed and thought about her latest adventure. As nice as it was to go down the stairs into new and exciting places, she was getting a bit tired of having to come back to the real world, where she was so unhappy. She loved all the experiences she had been having, but truly wished that her real life could be as wonderful as the one she had below the stairs.

It used to be like that, when Jade was her friend and Kimberly wasn't in the picture. She had always been content.

Of course, she had still hated Math, but it didn't matter as much if she could talk about it with Jade. At least the stairs under her bed were keeping her busy, and she hadn't had any time to mess up her room again.

Stacy got down on her knees and peered under the bed at the trap door. *Maybe I should stop going down there,* she thought to herself. Stacy was getting worried because every time she went down the stairs, had a wonderful adventure, and came back up again, her real life seemed to get worse and worse. It was as boring and sad as ever. But Stacy didn't want to give up her adventures completely either. *Maybe I'll just stop going every single night,* she thought as she got back to her feet. *I'll try and have more fun up here.* But that was going to be awfully hard to do without Jade.

CHAPTER TEN

The next morning Stacy thought about her decision to go down the stairs less often, and wondered what she could do instead that evening. That's when she realized that she had missed the SMILE concert on MTV last night. The adventures were definitely taking up too much time.

At school, Jade was waiting for Stacy in the parking lot. "Do you want to come to my house after school? My mom is baking your favourite chocolate chip cookies, and I thought we could watch the SMILE concert together. I recorded it last night because my dad was watching a baseball game. Did you see it?" Jade was smiling.

"No, I forgot. But I'd love to come! I haven't had your mom's cookies for a long time!" Stacy was thrilled. Maybe she wouldn't have to rely on the stairs for fun anymore!

"Okay, great! Kimberly and I are walking to my house after school. We can all go together!"

Stacy's smile fell off and splashed on the pavement. "What? Kimberly's coming?"

"Of course. She's my friend too, Stacy. I want us all to be friends!"

"I told you – I tried to be her friend yesterday, and she was horrible to me. I don't want to be her friend. I'll only come if she doesn't." Stacy marched away but stopped and turned back. "Besides, doesn't she have flute lessons, or ballet or dance or something?"

"No, she quit her flute lessons." Stacy thought about that. Maybe Kimberly's mom had finally listened to her and given her more time to do fun stuff. That must have made her happy. But it still didn't change the fact that Kimberly had been spiteful to her.

During the day, Stacy kept looking at Jade and remembering all their fun times together. If it meant having Jade to do things with again, Stacy thought that maybe she could give Kimberly another chance. She really wanted to go to Jade's, and if Kimberly was there, so what? At least she would get a chance to be with Jade again.

At lunch Stacy went over to sit with Kimberly and Jade, but when Kimberly saw Stacy coming, she packed up her lunch and dragged Jade, who was still eating her sandwich, onto the playground. *That's it*, Stacy thought. *I give up!* She ate her lunch with Trinh, Lacey and Christina, who told her all about the SMILE concert that she had missed.

After school, Stacy watched Jade and Kimberly leave together. Stacy was miserable and didn't feel like going home just yet, so she went out to the playground and sat on the swings. Usually she would be running home to get her homework done so she could race down the stairs into a new adventure. But she had promised herself to try and be satisfied with her real life, which meant staying away from the trap door. *But what will I do tonight? The only time I'm cheerful is when I open the trap door. I don't want to go home and think about Jade and Kimberly eating cookies together.*

After a few minutes on the swing, Stacy got up and started walking home. She was scowling. The only time she smiled anymore was when she thought of opening the trap door to see what was waiting for her...*I don't care*, Stacy thought to herself. *If I'm enjoying my adventures, then what's stopping me? There's nothing for me here. I might as well go down the stairs where I know*

SMILE

I will be happy.

When Stacy got home, she said hello to her mother and told her that she was going to go do her homework and would be back down for dinner. But Stacy had no intention of doing her homework just yet. She couldn't wait until after dinner to go down the stairs - she had to go now.

All she wanted was to forget about Jade and Kimberly and to smile again. So she moved the bed, opened the door and began her descent.

As Stacy took her first few steps, tears began to roll down her face. She wished with all her heart that she was in Jade's kitchen, with Jade, her mom and maybe even Kimberly. But that wasn't going to happen, so Stacy wiped her tears and kept moving down the stairs. When she got to the bottom, she found a closed door. Not sure what to do, she knocked and waited.

There was no answer. She knocked again. When nothing happened, she reached out and tried the handle, which turned easily. It was unlocked. Stacy took a deep breath and pushed the door open.

When she saw where the door led, she almost started crying again. School! She was at school! Stacy was angry; she came down the stairs to have fun, not to go back to school. It looked as if the day was just about to start, so she closed the door behind her and went to take her seat.

Much to Stacy's surprise, there was already someone sitting in her seat – her! Stacy could see herself sitting at her desk, flipping through a book and looking up towards the door. One of her classmates walked right in front of Stacy, so close that he almost knocked her over. *It must be like the time I was in Kimberly's house*, thought Stacy. *No one can see me here either.*

The classroom door opened again and Jade walked in. She ran over to Stacy's desk and put a small paper bag in front of her. "Here are your cookies! They're extra good this time!" Jade went to sit down just as Kimberly opened the classroom door and walked in, and headed straight to Stacy's desk just as Jade had done. Stacy watched Kimberly pick up the bag of cookies and hold them to her nose.

"These smell so good!" said Kimberly.

"You'll have to wait until lunch Kim; we can have them for dessert!" Stacy watched herself say. *What? Why would I be sharing my cookies with Kimberly? And why am I calling her Kim?*

The bell rang and everyone took his or her seat as Miss Terrence started the first lesson. Stacy watched in amazement as the three girls kept looking at each other and smiling. Everyone looked so happy. When the lesson ended and recess began, the three girls joined hands and ran out onto the playground. Stacy followed in disbelief.

As they were running towards the swings, Stacy watched herself trip and scrape her knee. "Are you okay?" Kimberly asked. She looked very troubled.

"I'm fine," Stacy heard herself say. "It's just a little scrape."

"Jade, go tell the teacher and I'll take her to the nurse to get a band-aid."

"It's okay, Kim! Really!"

"Well, we'd better get it cleaned anyway. It's starting to bleed. Come with me."

Stacy watched Jade run back to the school, while she and Kimberly headed towards the nurse's room, hand in hand. Kimberly was being so nice to Stacy – what was going on?

The next lesson passed by very quickly and it was soon time for lunch. Stacy walked into the lunchroom and saw herself sitting with Jade, Kimberly, Trinh, Christina and Lacey. All six girls were laughing and talking, and Stacy watched herself give Kimberly one of her precious cookies. After the girls had finished eating, they raced out onto the playground, Kimberly with her arm around Stacy's shoulder. She was having a hard time walking with her scraped knee and Kimberly was supporting her. As Stacy watched this, she was touched. *If only Kimberly were like that in real life,* she thought.

After school was over, Stacy watched herself, Jade and Kimberly skip to the parking lot where Kim's mom was waiting in a fancy black car. "I'll see you tonight!" Kimberly said to

SMILE

Jade and Stacy, giving them each a quick hug.

"Good luck, Kim, in case we don't see you before the show starts!" Stacy watched herself say.

"You'll be the best ballet dancer on the stage! I know it!" said Jade. It seemed to Stacy that she and Jade had plans to watch Kimberly's ballet recital that night. None of this was making sense to her.

The real Stacy walked back to the playground, sat down on the swings, and thought about the discovery of the trap door under her bed. She had found the stairs just as she started feeling unhappy, so she assumed that they came into her life to give her something to smile about. But now the stairs weren't leading her to happiness at all. She was right back in the middle of her regular life. Well, almost regular. It looked like a lot of things had changed, but Stacy wasn't sure she liked those changes. She closed her eyes and tried to think about why she might be here.

In every other adventure, Stacy had learned something and had fun at the same time. In the ocean she learned about sea creatures and enjoyed swimming around with them. When she was a member of SMILE she learned that it was hard work to be a pop star, but she enjoyed the one concert she had given. In London she had learned so much about the city and what it was like to be in another country. It had all been so much fun! Even when she was in Ancient Greece learning about the first Olympics, she'd had fun with the Goddess Athena.

Stacy wasn't entirely sure what she'd learned from her visit to Kimberly's, except that she was able to see that Kimberly wasn't perfect; she gets lonely and glum sometimes, like anyone else. In the rainforest she'd learned to fly and encountered amazing scenery and creatures, but what was she supposed to learn here, in her real life?

When Stacy opened her eyes again, she was shocked to see that she was back in her own home. Instead of sitting on the swing, she was sitting on the sofa in her living room and Stacy saw something even more surprising right in front of her.

Kimberly was in the Myers' house! Right in her living room. Stacy could see herself sitting on the floor next to Kimberly, playing a game on the Wii. It looked like Stacy was winning, but Kimberly was laughing and it looked like they were both having a great time. *Why do I look so happy?* Stacy thought. Whenever Kimberly was around, Stacy was usually grimacing, not grinning.

Stacy did win the game, and when she won, Kimberly surprised her by saying, "That's it! I give up! I won two and you won two. Let's call a truce!" That wasn't like the Kimberly she knew. The old Kimberly would have begged to play another game so she could beat Stacy, not tie with her. She couldn't understand why Kimberly was acting the way she was. And where was Jade? Why was Kimberly at Stacy's house alone? Stacy's head was spinning. She closed her eyes and shook her head.

When she opened her eyes, she discovered that she was no longer in her living room, but in Kimberly's. She could see Jade, Kim, and herself sitting on one of the big leather couches under a big, soft blanket. The three girls were sharing a giant bowl of popcorn. Sandra, the babysitter, was sprawled on another sofa and they were all watching a movie on Kimberly's huge TV.

When the movie ended, Sandra said, "Kimberly – you promised you'd help Stacy with her math homework and then it's time for bed." The three girls protested, but eventually made their way up the stairs to Kimberly's pink bedroom. Jade picked up a book and sat on Kimberly's bed reading, and Stacy watched herself and Kimberly sit down at the desk with their math books. Their heads were bent over the books, and their pencils were scribbling away for a long time.

"There!" said Kimberly. "Got it?"

"I think so!" Stacy watched herself say. "You're the best Kim! Thanks!"

From downstairs came Sandra's voice, "I'm coming up in five minutes! If you're not in bed, there'll be no popcorn the next time we watch a movie together!" Stacy watched as they all hopped into the huge bed and pulled the covers over their heads. She could hear a lot of giggling and whispering, but she couldn't make out what they were saying.

They're having so much fun, Stacy thought. *Wait – no! **I'm** having so much fun. With Jade. And Kimberly. Maybe that's what I'm supposed to learn here. That Kimberly can be my friend, and that real life can be just as good as the adventures under the stairs.* She looked back towards the bed as a giant wave of laughter erupted from under the covers. *Maybe even better...*

Sandra came in, told the girls to be quiet, flicked off the light and closed the door. As soon as she was gone, the whispers and giggles returned. Stacy smiled. She suddenly knew what she had to do. She walked out of the room, down the stairs and closed her eyes when she reached the bottom. When she opened them again, she was right where she wanted to be, at the bottom of the stairs under the trap door. She bounded up to her room, put everything back in order and went down for dinner.

"Mom," Stacy said as she sat down at the table, "can I invite two friends over after school tomorrow?"

"Sure, honey. Who?"

"Jade and Kimberly."

Her mom looked surprised. "I thought Jade wasn't your friend anymore, and that you didn't like Kimberly."

"Well, I miss Jade a lot and I don't think I really know Kimberly all that well. She might be okay."

"Well, I'm proud of you Stacy. It's very grown up of you to give Kimberly a chance like that. I'll bet you'll be surprised. Kimberly is probably a very nice girl."

Stacy smiled. "I think she probably is!"

As soon as dinner was over, Stacy ran upstairs and dialled Jade's number. Jade answered on the first ring. "Hello?"

"Jade, it's me."

"Stacy. You should have come over for cookies. We had a really good time."

"I know. I was being stupid."

"You're not stupid! Maybe a bit crazy, but not stupid!" Jade laughed.

"I'm sorry!"

"Sorry for what? For being crazy?"

"No. For being silly about Kimberly. I want to give her another chance. I know we can all be friends."

"Really?"

"Yes, really! My mom said that you and Kimberly could come over to my house after school tomorrow. That way I can get to know Kimberly a bit better. Do you think she'll want to come?"

"I know she will. I'll call her now and tell her. We'll see you at school tomorrow. Okay?"

"Great!" Stacy paused. "Jade?"

"What is it?"

"I really missed you."

"I know. I missed you too."

Stacy woke up the next day with butterflies in her stomach. What if Kimberly didn't want to come over? What if they didn't get along? But Stacy knew that she had to try. It was critical.

When she got to school, Jade and Kimberly were waiting for her at the school gates. Stacy's heart was fluttering as she walked over to them. "Hi," she said.

"Hi," chorused Jade and Kimberly.

Stacy looked at Kimberly and was relieved to see her smiling. "Can you come to my house after school, Kimberly?"

"Yes, I can."

"Good. I'm glad."

"Me too. Stacy?"

"Yeah?" Stacy felt nervous when she heard Kimberly's voice quiver.

"I'm sorry that I was mean to you before. I just...well I

thought you were going to take Jade away from me. I don't have very many true friends and I didn't want to lose her."

"Well, I guess I was kind of trying to take her away from you. I wanted Jade all to myself."

"So did I!" They both laughed.

"That was ridiculous. I'm sure we can all be friends," Stacy said.

"I know we can!" shouted Jade, hugging both of her friends. "Hooray!"

"Stacy, one more thing," said Kimberly, putting her hands on her hips.

Uh oh, thought Stacy, here we go. "Yeah?"

"Call me Kim."

Stacy let out big sigh of relief and smiled. "No problem!"

The day passed so quickly that Stacy barely had time to think about her new friend. She felt so pleased about getting to know Kim that she was finally able to concentrate on her lessons. She didn't have anything to worry about anymore. At lunch, Jade and Kim sat with Stacy, Trinh, Christina and Lacey before they all played a game of tag on the playground. At first Trinh looked surprised that Kim was sitting with them, but Kim cracked a joke almost as soon as she sat down and everyone laughed and relaxed.

School finally ended and Jade and Kim walked to Stacy's house with her. "What are we going to do at your house, Stacy?" Kim asked.

"We can play Wii, or go bike riding or play a game on Stacy's computer," Jade said. "There's a lot to do at Stacy's!"

"No! There's something much better we can do. I have something exciting to show you!" Stacy said impulsively. Jade and Kim exchanged puzzled glances.

When they arrived at Stacy's house, her mom was waiting

for them at the door. "Hello, Jade! Nice to see you again," she said. "And you must be Kimberly!"

"Yes," said Kim, somewhat shyly.

The three girls followed Mrs. Myers into the house. "Have fun, girls!"

"We'll be in my room, Mom." Stacy turned to Jade and Kim and said, "Ready?"

They nodded and Stacy led them up to her room and shut the door behind them. To Jade she said, "Can you help me move my bed?"

"Move your bed? Why?"

"You'll see!" Stacy said with a devious smile. Stacy and Jade pushed the bed out of the way while Kim watched them with interest.

Once the bed was out of the way, Stacy looked down at the bare floor, but there was no trap door. "Oh!" she said, in surprise.

"What is it?" asked Kim.

Stacy was so shocked that she just gawked at her two friends with her mouth hanging open.

"Stacy usually has a really messy room. There's always a big mess under her bed," Jade said to Kim. Turning to Stacy, she continued, "That's really great, Stacy. I've never seen your room this clean! Is that what you wanted to show us?"

"Um," said Stacy, still confused. "Um. No! That's it - your birthday present, I mean, I thought it was hiding under the bed, but I guess I put it away, now that I'm tidy and all," Stacy managed to get out. To conceal her bewilderment, Stacy put on her favourite SMILE CD, went over to her dresser and opened the top drawer. She pulled out the birthday present and handed it to Jade. She was smiling the whole time, but inside, her brain was screaming. Where was the trap door? What was she going to do now? Had she imagined the whole thing?

She looked over at Jade and Kim who were regarding her curiously. After Jade opened her present and hugged Stacy in thanks, they moved the bed back in place and sat down on it together. The three girls sang along to the music and relaxed against the pillows.

I guess it doesn't really matter, Stacy thought, as she bopped to the music with Jade and Kim. *I don't need the stairs anymore. I have Jade back, and better yet - now I have Kim too! There's plenty to smile about in real life.* Looking at her two good friends, she sat up, smiled a genuine smile and said, "Well, what do you want to do now?"

ABOUT THE AUTHOR

Dawnelle Salant is a freelance travel writer and children's author. Growing up in the resort town of Fernie, B.C., Dawnelle always expressed a desire to see the rest of the world. A Language Arts/ESL Education Degree from the University of Calgary enabled Dawnelle to pursue her love of travel while realizing her dream of working with children. To date, she has spent eight years traveling the world and teaching in international schools in Guatemala, England, Turkey and Australia.

While exploring the world as an English teacher, Dawnelle became interested in travel publications. Her love for writing developed as she searched for ways to share her remarkable experiences with family, friends, and eventually, the rest of the world. Writing children's books has given her an opportunity to combine her passion for writing with her love for children and her teaching career. Dawnelle has recently returned to Canada after traveling Australia and New Zealand for almost two years. She is currently teaching Grade 3 in Calgary. *Smile* is her first novel for children.